Big George and the Winter King

Eric Pringle

illustrated by
Colin Paine

BLOOMSBURY
CHILDREN'S
BOOKS

To Pat – My Wife, Inspiration and Best Friend – EP
For Leo – CP

First published in Great Britain in 2004 by Bloomsbury Publishing Plc
38 Soho Square, London, W1D 3HB

ISBN 0 7475 6341 1

Designed and typeset by Tracey Cunnell
Printed in Great Britain by Clays Ltd, St Ives plc

1 3 5 7 9 10 8 6 4 2

All papers used by Bloomsbury Publishing are natural, recyclable products made
from wood grown in well-managed forests. The manufacturing processes conform
to the environmental regulations of the country of origin.

contents

	Foreword: Whispers from Space	7
1	A Stranger in a Very Strange Land	9
2	Follow that Star	15
3	Village in the Hills	19
4	The Boy at the Window	25
5	Grolyhoomp	31
6	Count Your Blessings	41
7	Sorcerer	47
8	Séance on a Sunny Afternoon	53
9	Boy Bess	63
10	The Grolyhoomp Song	69
11	It's a Wonder	77
12	George in the Dark	87
13	S O S	97
14	Cockatrice	101
15	It's a Knock-Out	113
16	Potion	121
17	Who Will Be Crowned?	129
18	King for a Day or Two	141
19	Sir Solomon	147
20	Reunion	155

21	George in Danger	159
22	One Good Turn	165
23	Action Grolyhoomp	171
24	George Gets Mad	177
25	Miracle at Kingswell	187
26	The Spirit of Christmas	197
27	Something Has Changed	203
	Afterword	207

Foreword

Whispers from Space

Although Time stands almost still on Halrig, Big George's home star in the far constellation of Ursa Middling, on Earth it flows like a river, drowning year after year.

George sleeps on regardless, snoring like a hundred oinking pigs inside the hill that protects him. And as he sleeps, the Fourteenth Century steals by. Earth grows older but no wiser.

In England people are born, live their lives, and die. Kings and Queens come and go. Not long ago plague visited the countryside so savagely it almost emptied it of people, so that whole towns and villages had to start all over again. On Planet Earth there are always upheavals.

Even so, around Big George's hill the seasons pass serenely by. The wild rose on its summit, planted in George's memory hundreds of years ago by Tilly Miller, still bursts into leaf each spring, flowers in summer and fades in autumn. Then winter freezes the soil so hard you would think nothing could grow in it any more. But next year the rose will bloom again. It always does.

All this time Big George whistles and blows in his sleep and the rabbit's foot pinned to his tunic by Joanne of Nowhere rises and falls, rises and falls.

Here in his bedroom everything seems changeless.

But it is not.

Imagine.

Time on Planet Earth has reached December in the Year of Our Lord 1399 – two hundred and ninety-six years since Big George's spacecraft fizzed through our atmosphere and crashed into an English forest, wiping out his memory.

Not far away, in the border region between England and Wales known as the Marchlands, a Welshman called Owain Glyndwr has been making such a nuisance of himself that the newly-crowned English King Henry the Fourth has sent an army from London to teach him a lesson.

It is a very small and ill-equipped army, which only yesterday marched raggedly past Big George's hill. He didn't hear them, of course.

This mysterious borderland, this country of mists and mountains, is a strange and magical place hinged between two countries and really belonging to neither. And on these December nights, hinged between two centuries, the magic seems so strong that people cross their hearts and fingers and believe that anything can happen.

Everybody is nervous. The soldiers, the Welsh, the English and the March people alike all look for omens and signs. They find plenty, though none is quite as magical as the vision which has begun to appear in the night sky: a fiery comet, blazing westward and trailing a ribbon of light. That, the people say, foretells a miracle.

For once they're right: two miracles are going to happen here very soon.

One of them is called George.

chapter one

∧ Stranger in a very Strange Land

In December 1399 a great freeze gripped the Marchlands between England and Wales. The cold reached into the most unlikely places until finally it pushed its icy fingers right through the clods of Big George's hill and touched the sleeping figure inside.

It painted a silver coating over the message pinned to his chest and the rabbit's foot beside it. It froze his beard, dimmed the green light that glowed in his cheeks and stiffened his boots to stone.

Attacked by the frost from all sides, George shivered in his sleep. Icicles pricked his eyebrows like needles. He tried to brush them away but his fingers wouldn't move.

The effort roused him. He sat up stiffly and sleepily. He blinked into the darkness beyond the range of his cheeks' emerald glow. He flapped his arms and hugged himself. 'Grolyhoomp,' he muttered through lips frozen hard as bricks. 'Snik-backer-wigglo!' – 'Hello! My, but it's cold!'

He yawned and his breath steamed.

Creakily George rose to his feet. He thought it might be less cold outside, so he pressed his shoulder against the hinged wall. It opened slowly, dislodging clods that slithered down his neck like nuggets of ice.

George crawled through, took a look outside – and gasped with surprise.

Although it was night, after the deeper darkness of his bedroom he could make out the shapes of bushes and straggly trees. All were rigid with the frost, which on this December night was a living thing that clamped chilly fingers over George's face and body and made his long locked neck stiffer than ever.

It certainly was not warmer out here, but George hardly felt the cold now. All his attention was given to the sky. It brimmed with stars. Above his head the Milky Way shimmered. To his left and right galaxies stretched to the horizon. And moving westward with an almost visible motion was a most extraordinary comet trailing a white ribbon of light.

George gazed entranced.

And he listened.

It seemed as if the stars spoke to him. The galaxies sang. The Milky Way hummed. The comet whispered, 'Look at me. Watch me. Follow me – follow my tail!'

Watching it, listening to it, something exciting happened to George. Inside his damaged memory he felt a small – a very small – shift ... as if a key was opening, very slightly, a forgotten door.

He had no idea what lay at the other side of the door, but the very fact of it opening at all delighted him beyond measure.

It gave him hope. Because to lose your memory is a strange and terrible thing.

When Big George cracked his head during his landing on Earth, he lost all connection with the things which, until then, had made him real to himself.

He no longer knew who he was.

He did not know where he was.

He did not know where he had come from, or why he was here.

And to add to his misfortunes, when he met the people who lived in this world he couldn't understand a word they said.

Big George, in fact, was as lost as you can possibly be.

But George was not stupid. Far from it. He looked for clues and pointers. He tried to learn the people's language by mimicking the sounds their words made. He looked inside their heads and hearts to understand how they thought and felt. But even so, after two unforgettable adventures, he was still not much further forward.

The problem was it was bedtime on Halrig. George should be asleep now. But he had learned to his cost that if he nodded off around here, when he woke everything would be changed.

He had lost Tilly Miller and Simpkin Sampkins that way and now, crouching outside his hill, sniffing the starlit land, he knew that another change had taken place. Which meant that his new friends Walter of Swyre and Joanne of Nowhere would also have disappeared.

Here people came and went like dust on the wind. That was confusing.

It was also bewildering that among all the people he had met none looked anything like himself. He was a stranger in a very strange land.

Yet now, suddenly and unexpectedly, the comet had spoken to him.

'Follow me,' it had whispered.

George stood up. 'All right,' he said to himself, 'that's what I'll do. I'll follow that star. And while I'm following it I'll learn about this place – I'll look and listen, see and find. That will be an adventure!'

He knew he would have to be careful, though, because up to now nearly everybody he'd met had been unfriendly.

There seemed no one he could trust. Because who can you turn to when there's no one else like you in the world?

Fired with this new purpose, George stood up tall and straight.

Stretching his cramped muscles he unfolded himself until he towered higher than any tree in the forest.

For one last moment he waited, tasting the air and savouring it.

Then, closing his ears to the clanging universe and trusting a comet to guide him, he strode away into the winter night, heading westward.

chapter Two

Follow that Star

As Big George began his journey he eagerly looked for things to learn. What he found first was a puzzle – a puzzle about all the changes that had come over the world since he was last awake.

Then there had been birds, flowers, leaves, sunshine and soft warm air. Now, as a new day slowly dawned and the comet and the glow in his cheeks faded, George saw a grey, bleak land in the grip of bitter winter. The trees were leafless skeletons, black and still. There were no flowers and no colours. Birds were silent. Instead of comforting softness, the air pinched his face like the nails of a bad-tempered child and the ground rang hard as iron under his tramping feet.

Having no experience of winter, because on

Halrig there are no seasons, George thought that Earth had been stricken by a terrible disease, and was dying.

He worried about that a lot, until he heard a distant beating of drums. He ducked down behind a copse, peered warily round it and saw that ahead the flat lands he'd been crossing were giving way to low hills rising to a misty horizon.

And he saw that climbing the nearest hill, and moving westward like himself, was a small army.

A drummer led the way, sounding a rhythmical, hypnotic beat. Behind him an untidy line of soldiers shuffled like a column of weary ants. Half a dozen were on horseback while the rest slogged it on foot.

George's concern was to pass the ramshackle army unseen, so he waited until it was out of sight and then, keeping low, wheeled northward to circle the hill.

But when you're a forty-foot-high grolyhoomp it's hard to be invisible, and even though George crouched as low as he could without actually toppling over, his head and shoulders were for a few moments clearly visible to the drummer, who was a little ahead of the rest.

George forged on, unaware he had been seen but aware that the drummer had missed a beat. If he had turned he would have seen that the tiny man had become a pale and shaking wreck, certain he had seen his first Welsh monster, and convinced that this trip was going to turn out badly.

In that he was quite right.

All that day the monotonous drumming echoed inside George's head. All day he marched westward, through a country ever more disturbed by hills. He saw no one else because the local people, farmers all, were keeping to their hearth-fires. Cultivation was impossible in weather like this.

He heard a few sounds, though: an axe chopping wood, a shepherd calling his sheep, a dog barking – and once, far away, a cockerel crowing like a wailing bagpipe and making the lonely land seem even more lonely.

At least, thought George, the sounds proved that the land wasn't quite dead yet.

In the afternoon he reached a river that gleamed a dull pewter in the fading light. Although it was wide the water was low and George was able to cross it by jumping from island to island, cracking and crunching ice-floes to powder beneath his great boots.

After the river the hills grew higher and closer together with deep narrow valleys between, so that from a distance the country looked as if dozens of whales had beached themselves there.

Dusk was short and swift. The stars pricked out again and in the western sky the comet sailed into view, showing George the way to go.

He adjusted his direction slightly.

When it was almost too dark to see the ground beneath his feet, he reached the summit of the highest hill of all – and noticed two things.

The first, far below, was a ring of light made by the clustering fires and candles of a small village.

The other was even more unexpected: George noticed that high above the village and his own head the comet had stopped moving.

chapter Three

Village in the Hills

On that bleak midwinter evening the village of Kingswell – crouched beneath a mountain with a comet hovering above – looked like a scene from a Christmas carol. (Think 'Good King Wenceslas' and you'll be very close.)

A small stone church with a wooden tower was perched on a hump of ground scattered with yew trees. Below it houses, farms and barns huddled together for company.

On another rocky hump a fortified manor reared like a black fist. It was more castle than house, and at this windless hour the flag on its battlements hung limply. All of its windows were dark except one, where a torch weakly flared.

To George on his cold hilltop the lights of Kingswell seemed to twinkle like stars, as if the village was the centre of its own small universe. That was also exactly how its inhabitants thought of it, because if you lived in Kingswell everywhere else was a very long way off.

It could stay there too, the villagers thought, because in their experience the outside world brought nothing but trouble. Why, only a few decades ago had it not sent the plague, whose effects were all too visible in the churchyard? And now there were rumours that the English king was sending soldiers to wreak more havoc on their innocent heads, as punishment for the behaviour of that rebellious Welshman, Owain Glyndwr.

What had Kingswell to do with a Welsh prince? Or an English King? A curse on both their countries, for Kingswell was neither Welsh nor English, look you, and didn't want to be either.

Besides, it had enough troubles of its own already.

Why, had not its lord, Sir Simeon Griphook, become such a weeping baby since his poor wife died that he had completely lost his grip on the village and now seemed to be losing his wits?

And was not his daughter, the motherless Bess, miserably unhappy to see her father and Kingswell sinking under the ruthless sway of Solomon Sneck the Sorcerer?

And was not that sorcerer hungry for more and

more power, until it seemed he would not be satisfied until he had all of Kingswell crushed inside his bony fist?

And did not everybody else have troubles, right down to the lowest of the low – to Huw Evans the pig boy, who was unhappy because he had no power at all and no authority, even over his pigs?

With all that going on, the villagers whispered around their winter fires, they needed an invading army like a hole in the head. Why, they grumbled, crossing themselves superstitiously as they spoke, they would rather be visited by a monster, or a giant!

If those villagers had looked outside at that moment they'd have thought their wish had been granted for, high above them on the mountain, George's face was glowing like a green cheese moon, and his shape – which could have been a man's if it had not possessed a swan's neck and been so utterly huge – reared up gigantically against the stars like their worst nightmare.

And now that nightmare was moving – descending – heading their way!

George, who ever since he landed on Earth had been looking for somewhere to belong, decided to look into Kingswell – and listen and learn and seek and find.

But as he made his way down the mountain by the light of his cheeks he felt anxious, as we all do when we're entering the unknown.

For George, everything and everywhere was unknown.

When he reached the village he heard music. From the dark manor there came the soft twanging of a harp, accompanying a lilting voice which chanted words that were neither song nor speech but something in between.

Walking tiptoe ('dibdoo' he called it), George was able to approach the manor unseen and unheard. But as he neared the lighted window, which had been opened to let out the smoke from the fire inside, he stopped sharply.

Because outside the window, peering inside and listening enthralled to the chanting, there was a boy.

chapter Four

The Boy at the window

Huw Evans had a dream.

It came to him every morning when, at first light, he woke on his straw pallet in the cowshed which had served his family for a house since the day his father died.

Lying very still, he dreamed that this was the day when the fabulous Great Hero of Kingswell would return and transform him from a pig boy to something altogether wonderful.

In his dream Huw saw the Hero quite clearly: a massive red-bearded giant who rode full tilt out of the west with the setting sun turning his head to flame. He came for one purpose only – to touch Huw's starving family with magic and change their lives for ever.

Tears of longing scalded his eyelids. 'It *could*

happen!' he told himself. 'It isn't impossible because it happened once before, right here in Kingswell. And anything that has happened once can happen again!'

That was why Huw was trespassing here now, risking discovery, clinging to ivy outside the manor hall window, shivering with cold and eavesdropping on the people who – all except one – despised him.

Inside the hall, by the flickering light from torch and fire, a minstrel was chanting the Legend of the Winter King.

He was an old man, well past eighty, but as he sang he moved nimbly about the hall, stepping lightly between sleeping dogs and the sprawling legs of his audience, who had heard the story many times before but never tired of hearing it again.

'From the western lands in the hour of our need
Rode a King who would answer our prayers indeed
And set our people free…'

He paused and looked round the room to make sure everyone was awake for the climax of his story.

Near the fire the languid frame of Sir Simeon Griphook stiffened with anticipation.

At his knees the small figure of his daughter Bess tensed, her dark curls and eyes shining brightly in the firelight.

Close by, the crouching form of Solomon Sneck stirred, unhooked itself like a straightening question mark, then hunched back again.

Beyond them, away from the fire, the worthy people of Kingswell clustered like ghosts in the shadows, holding their breath.

The minstrel was satisfied. He could end his tale.
'See the villains flee before him!
See their blood on his sword and spear!
See the glory of the sun shine round him
Shielding him from hurt and fear..!'

Huw's knuckles tightened round the ivy. Once again in his mind's eye he saw the mysterious Hero who, centuries ago, had visited a village called Simonswell to free it from oppression. After a wonderful victory he had disappeared as quickly as he came, but he left behind a hope that should the need arise again another King, another Giant, would come riding out of the sunset to perform miracles of daring.

In gratitude, and to ensure that the story would never be forgotten, the villagers had done two things.

First, they renamed their village Kingswell.

Second, they established the annual Ceremony of the Winter King, during which a simple soul was crowned King for the season and honoured as the Spirit of Christmas.

The custom was still going strong and the people of Kingswell felt sure that this year it would be more important than it had ever been before. As soon as the minstrel had ended his song their mutterings began.

'We should start praying for that King to come

back before those English soldiers get here!'

'That's only a rumour. There may be no soldiers at all.'

'Even if there are,' said a third man, a swarthy fellow with a squint who scratched his nose incessantly, 'they mayn't find us. We're not easy to find.'

Then they began to worry about the terrifying things that were foretold to happen as the old century died and the new one reared over the horizon.

'We've got all that coming to us, see, as well as the soldiers. Dragons rising from the earth.'

'Griffins diving from the clouds, breathing fire.'

'Black poison flowing across the ground and turning your feet to mush.'

'What are we going to do?'

'What *can* we do?'

'We can pray, that's all. Pray for that King to come, look you.'

Huw was afraid. He was scared by the rumours of ruthless soldiers seeking revenge. He was worried by the superstitious talk because he was sure it would all come true.

And he trembled at the sight of Solomon Sneck the Sorcerer unwinding his lumpy frame again and shouting, in the harsh reedy voice that sounded half sneer and half threat, 'Newt's ears! I could solve all your problems with spells, if only...'

He stopped and stared insolently at the lord of the manor.

Sir Simeon Griphook returned his stare with a listless gaze. 'If only what, Solomon?'

The enchanter smiled. 'If only you'd give me the power I seek, my lord. If only you'd say the word.'

Bess Griphook clutched her father's arm. 'Don't listen to him!' she cried. 'Everything he says is a lie!'

Huw heard no more. He saw the malice slide across Solomon Sneck's eyes but then his fingers, numb with cold, slipped out of the ivy and he fell heavily to the ground.

The fall knocked the breath out of him. As he lay there Huw thought despairingly of his mother and sister huddling with the animals for warmth. And in his heart he knew that even though this winter was so bitter, and the loss of his father so great, the Hero of his dream would never come.

'Dreams are useless,' he thought. 'And stupid. Because why would a King come to a cowshed?'

Sighing, the Kingswell pig boy struggled to his feet, turned for home – and in a flash of green light had a *real* vision for the first time in his life.

chapter Five

Grolyhoomp

Huw yelled with fright.

He knew he shouldn't do that because he'd give himself away, but seeing the unbelievable bulk of Big George hiding the stars and lighting the air around with his eerily glowing face, he couldn't help it.

He also felt that praying for a giant to come had been a very bad mistake.

He yelped again when George leaned down over him and grinned. His cry startled a dog, which began to howl, and that disturbed another dog further off, whose barking roused ten more dogs and every cat in Kingswell. In no time there was such a hullabaloo that the guard on the manor battlements woke up and called out in drowsy alarm, 'Who goes there? Show yourself! Who goes there!'

Huw fled. He ran from giant, guard, dragons, griffins, dogs, cats and the cold snake eyes of Solomon Sneck.

But he got nowhere at all because after only two steps he tripped on a rusty chain lying across the manor drawbridge and fell into the moat.

He was sinking in icy slime when a hand the size of a horse plucked him out and set him dripping on the bank.

Huw coughed up something nasty and croaked,

'Don't kill me, please, I'm needed at home! Don't rob me, because I've got nothing! Don't frighten me, because I'm a coward!'

The giant lowered his face to see Huw clearly and frowned.

Huw, looking a sickly shade of green and feeling even sicker, thought he should give a reason why his life should be spared.

'You see, sir,' he babbled, 'two months ago my father was

chopping trees for Solomon Sneck – he's our landlord – when a tree fell on him. Father died, and because we were no use to Sneck any more he turned us out of our house and made us live in the cowshed.'

Talking about his family's misfortunes made Huw want to cry again.

'I look after Solomon Sneck's pigs, see,' he sniffed, 'but now it's winter they can find hardly any food. It's the coldest weather anyone can remember and *we've* got nothing to eat either, except what I can beg or steal and what Bess brings us – Bess is my friend, though her father would be mad if he knew she was friends with a pig boy.

'There's three of us at home, sir,' he babbled on, for now Huw had started he didn't seem able to stop. 'There's me, my sister Rachel, who's three, and my mother Sarah. Mother's going to have another baby soon, so she's hungry all the time. And she's not strong, and I'm frightened for her, sir, very frightened. So don't kill me, please – I'm needed!'

Breathless after the longest speech he had ever made, Huw Evans gazed up at the glowing giant. The giant looked baffled.

Huw cleared his throat.

'Beg pardon, sir,' he said, very slowly and clearly, 'do you understand what I'm saying?'

George lowered his face even closer. Pointing to himself, he opened his mouth and let out a noise that sounded like a beehive.

'Gg-eee-orr-ggge,' he said.

'Pardon?'

'Grolyhoomp.'

'Wh-who are you, sir?'

'Geeorrgge.'

George thought he was getting the hang of the language – people kept saying 'George' to him so it seemed friendly to say it back.

He wanted to be friendly.

Huw peered at the notice on the giant's tunic.

'If found. This is George,' he read. 'He is a grolyhoomp. Signed, Tilly Miller.'

'I'm Huw,' he said.

'Hooooooooo.'

Huw blinked. This must be somebody's idea of a joke. Warily he rose to his feet and backed away inch by inch. Then he turned and ran. After a while he looked round to see if the joke had gone. It hadn't. It was following him.

'Wicle snokrig, flimmernoot,' George buzzed. 'Carry on, boy.'

Suddenly and inexplicably, Huw felt happy. The grolyhoomp's enormous grin made him want to laugh for the first time since his father died. What a wonder he'd found! People whispered about dragons and griffins but *he* had found a grolyhoomp! Wait till Mother and Rachel saw him!

In his excitement Huw ran even faster, with George following dibdoo in his shed-sized boots.

And that is how it happened that Huw the pig boy arrived home with magic at his heels.

When Rachel saw George she screamed. You can understand why. There's big – there's very big – there's colossal – and then in a different league altogether there is Big George. To a three-year-old girl looking anxiously for her brother through the cowshed's low doorway it seemed he was returning with the Devil at his heels.

Rachel's cry brought her mother scurrying, and when Sarah saw George she fainted.

Rachel screamed a second time, Huw ran into the cowshed in dismay, Rachel slammed the door shut – and George was left outside and on his own again.

Half an hour later Sarah Evans was conscious again – but very worried.

'You can't possibly keep him, Huw!' she cried. 'How could we feed him, for a start?'

Huw shrugged. 'Dunno, Ma.'

'He could eat a cow three times a day. Four cows, even.'

'Maybe he doesn't like cows.'

'Bet he likes pigs, though,' Rachel said, peeping through a window at George's enormous bulk. 'We've got pigs, Huwy.'

'They're not my pigs, are they?' Huw protested. 'They're Solomon Sneck's, and if that grolyhoomp so much as touches one Sneck will hang me up for meat myself!'

'Don't say that, Huwy! Don't say that!'

'So what I ask again,' murmured Sarah Evans weakly, 'is what on earth are we going to do with a grolyhoomp!'

If only they'd known, George wasn't hungry. You don't eat while you're asleep, and he was supposed to be asleep.

He was thirsty, though. He would have to have a drink soon.

Shivering with cold, he fingered the spoon in his pocket and the rabbit's foot on his chest and recalled Tilly's smile, Jo's spirit and Walter's courage.

He missed them a lot, and standing in the dark outside a rickety cowshed in another unknown place filled with strangers, he felt the all too familiar loneliness fall over him like a heavy cloak.

He sighed – then shrugged it off. 'No use moping,' he told himself. 'What good does it do? Look, listen, seek, find – that's the thing to do. And maybe when I've done it I'll belong here.'

That's what George was hoping as he stood in the darkness in this remotest of valleys, locked magically in no-man's land and no-man's time.

Magic really can happen in a circumstance like that, and George felt it hovering in the air around him like a presence that might show itself at any moment.

He became so sure it was going to happen *now* that he held his breath and waited for it.

And waited, forgetting to breathe again.

And still waited, holding that breath until he thought he would burst.

That is how things were at the cowshed when Bess Griphook, escaping from superstitious talk and the sinister presence of Solomon Sneck, arrived with a basket of food for her friends and met a grolyhoomp for the very first time.

chapter six

count your blessings

WHOOOOOSH!

The sound of Big George releasing the pent-up breath he could hold no longer would have beaten the biggest sneeze of all time by at least a thousand per cent.

It crossed the borderland into England like a hurricane, met the King's soldiers fifty miles away and knocked them down.

It blew Bess back through the gate she'd just come in by – but then George breathed in and sucked her back again.

A lot of girls would have wept in a situation like that, but Bess was no crybaby. Instead of weeping she lay on the ground with her eyes shut and counted her blessings.

'I'm still alive,' she thought. 'That's a top

blessing. I'm ten years old, tall, strong, skilled at music, dancing, horse-riding and embroidery – though I don't like that much. So what am I afraid of? I'm afraid of opening my eyes, that's what.'

Steeling herself, she squinted through trembling eyelids and saw Huw bending over her holding a lantern and looking worried, and behind him – a Thing.

'We heard the noise,' Huw said. 'It sounded as if the cowshed was falling down, so I came running. Are you all right?'

Gingerly Bess moved her arms and legs. 'I think so. But ...' she lowered her voice to a whisper ... 'what's *that?*'

'Ah.' Huw glanced over his shoulder and grinned. 'Bess, meet George.'

'George? That monster is called *George*?'

'Apparently.'

'What is he?'

Huw pointed to the notice. 'A grolyhoomp. That's what it says.'

'What's a grolyhoomp?'

'Dunno.'

Huw gazed apologetically at George. 'I'm sorry,' he said gently. 'I'll have to take Bess inside before she freezes. But I can't fit you in, can I? You'd raise the roof and squash the beasts. Don't go away, though.'

Huw helped Bess to her feet, led her inside and closed the door.

George smiled and kept on smiling. Only it wasn't a smile any more. His cheeks had frozen stiff.

Inside the cowshed cows stamped and pigs grunted and their breath steamed in the smoky light from the fire.

Bess choked on the acrid air. 'How could any man condemn people to live like this?' she wondered. 'And Huw's mother's going to have a baby. That man can do anything!'

It was Sneck Bess had come to talk about.

'He frightens me, Huw. He controls my father by pretending he can speak to my mother in the spirit world. He says she needs his help to reach Heaven – and Father believes him! He'll give that sorcerer anything he wants, so Sneck asks for property and power – he says the only way he can help my mother is by having more and more power himself every day!

'The way things are going he'll have our house soon, and then he'll be Lord of Kingswell and *we'll* live in a stinking cowshed like—'

Bess stopped. 'I'm sorry, I didn't mean that.'

'Yes, you did, child.'

Sarah Evans spoke quietly, glancing into the dark corners of her home where unseen creatures she didn't like to think about scuffled and squeaked.

'Do you think I don't feel as you do about this place? But I remind myself that once a miracle happened in a stable, and then it doesn't seem so bad.'

A spasm crossed her face and she closed her eyes. She was very tired.

Bess turned back to Huw and whispered, 'That man has so much to answer for. He trusts nobody, hates everybody – and he has eyes in the back of his head. He really is a sorcerer!'

'He told us he was when he first arrived here,'

Huw reminded her. 'Nobody knew where he came from but we were pleased to have him because we thought a sorcerer would protect us. Instead he uses his spells against us!'

Bess's dark eyes blazed with anger. 'We have to stop him. But how can we fight magic?'

Huw looked at the dwindling fire, the restless animals and his now-sleeping mother and sister. 'No use asking me, Bess. How could I defeat a sorcerer? I can't even feed my family.'

His gaze reached the window. It should have been black as the night outside, but as he looked it turned green.

*

George had been trying to warm himself up, blowing his cheeks to loosen them, flapping his arms to de-ice them and banging his feet on the hard ground like a musician clanging cymbals.

As he pranced about the farmyard he looked into a frozen cattle trough and saw a puckered, rumpled, palely shining face gazing back at him. For an instant the face reminded him of other faces – faces from long ago that were now forgotten and lost to him – still lost because that door which had opened a fraction refused to open further. The loneliness returned ten-fold, and for comfort he returned to the cowshed, knelt down and peered through the window.

His eyes met Huw's – and for a moment Huw could have sworn that the grolyhoomp was weeping.

chapter Seven

Sorcerer

In olden times people fully believed in things we don't believe in any more.

For example, they believed that the earth was flat and you could fall off the edge.

They certainly believed in the power of evil spirits, and all along the borderland there was absolute belief in witches, sorcerers and all kinds of magical goings on.

If you believe in something strongly enough, maybe it will happen.

If you really believe in fairies maybe you'll see them.

Look at it this way. Think of the twitching movements you could have sworn you saw in the hedge at the bottom of your garden, when you knew for certain there was no one there. And do you remember seeing curtains twitching in the window of an empty house – or the creaking sounds your own house makes when everybody is in bed?

Little things like that make you nervous and can easily cause you to believe that something supernatural is happening.

So what do you do?

You cross your fingers.

That, a million times stronger, is how the people of Kingswell felt in the dying days of 1399. They knew absolutely and for certain that evil spirits were lurking everywhere, like cats waiting to pounce.

Their fear was so strong that crossing their fingers was not enough. They needed much heavier protection – they needed a magician on their side.

It was just their bad luck that the magician the people of Kingswell got was Solomon Sneck the Sorcerer and Enchanter.

Sneck had once been a soldier in the army of the English King. He had not been a brave soldier, but during a skirmish with the Scots he had managed to save the King's life while actually trying to run away.

As a reward he was given a small piece of land on the Welsh border, next to the land belonging to Sir Simeon Griphook.

The thought of owning property went to Sneck's head and he came to Kingswell with the ambition of grabbing all the land and power there was to be had. He was an impatient man, and since he knew that achieving your ambition by fair means takes a long time, he chose foul.

He chose enchantment.

On the road to Kingswell he did several things he thought would help him on his way.

He changed his name from Simon to Solomon because he thought that made him sound less simple and more wise.

From a conjuror he discovered that the hand can be quicker than the eye.

From a soothsayer he learned hocus-pocus, which is the art of talking rubbish while making it sound perfectly sensible.

From a necromancer he acquired the know-how to recite spells that terrified and potions which smelled disgusting, and the knowledge that the more terrifying and disgusting he was the more people would pay.

He also bought herbs, spices, a cauldron, gunpowder to make flashes (flashes impress the customers, the necromancer told him) and a secret weapon to be used only in an emergency and handled with the greatest possible care.

Finally he stole a cloak and a pointed hat from a jester he met at a fair.

In this way Solomon Sneck came to Kingswell a fully qualified bogus sorcerer – small part conjuror, small part soothsayer, large part charlatan – and the most brazen liar in the country.

The first thing he did, without batting an eyelid, was to tell everybody he had been awarded his property for releasing the King from the spell of a wicked wizard by means of an even stronger spell of his own – and also for helping the Queen talk to her long-dead ancestors.

The people of Kingswell were impressed.

They were even more impressed when they saw Sneck in action.

They watched his frothing cauldron with popping eyes. They gasped at the explosions. They heard with awe the mumbo-jumbo with which he made balms for boils and carbuncles, the 'frogs' eyelashes, newts' ears and the 'smile of an unborn cat gathered precisely one hour before midsummer dawn'.

Sneck made it up as he went along, and like an actor hooked on applause he became addicted to his own performances and grew ever more melodramatic and outrageous.

So did his fees.

And he found that the necromancer had been correct: the more incredible the treatment, and the higher the price, the more the people of Kingswell believed in him.

Nobody believed more than Sir Simeon Griphook.

Bess's father missed his dead wife so much that when Sneck said it was possible to meet her in the spirit world he jumped for joy.

'I would give anything to contact my darling Mary again!' he cried. 'If you can speak to her you shall have whatever you desire!'

'Land,' said Sneck, sneering behind his sleeve at this sentimental fool. 'I desire land.'

He got it.

In séance after séance he pretended to enter the world of the dead and speak to Simeon's beloved Mary. Afterwards, overwhelmed by grief and joy, the tear-stained knight handed over a part of Kingswell.

At this rate the sorcerer would soon have more land than the lord of the manor himself. Eventually he would have it all.

But 'eventually' was not soon enough for the impatient Sneck. He wanted Kingswell, lock, stock and barrel, before the year was out.

There wasn't long to go…

chapter Eight

Séance on a Sunny Afternoon

On the afternoon following Big George's arrival, the weather changed and became less cold. The sun shone and the icicles hanging from the village roofs dripped like tears.

From his place of concealment in a copse behind the manor house (it had been Bess's idea to keep the grolyhoomp hidden as a possible secret weapon against Solomon Sneck) George peered through the winter trees and watched the daily life of Kingswell going on.

He saw Huw driving his pigs back from the forest where they'd been snuffling for acorns.

He saw the villagers at their winter tasks: chopping wood, salting meat, baking bread, making shoes and tools and clothes.

He saw labourers building a stockade against the threat of the approaching army.

He would have liked to help, but Bess said he should lie low. It seemed to George that he was always expected to stay out of sight and he wondered why.

Was he in danger – or dangerous?

Were people afraid of him?

If they were afraid, he thought, it could only be because they didn't know him. George didn't think he was frightening at all.

That was only one of the many puzzles about being on this planet. Another was going on inside the manor.

From the window of an upstairs room a high-pitched whining song reached him, accompanied by a peculiar smell which tickled his nose and made him want to sneeze.

George hoped he wouldn't, because his sneezes always had a devastating effect.

At this point the trees grew close to the manor wall. Gambling that no one would come round the back of the manor and see him, George inched forward, propped himself on an elbow and put an eye to the window.

Inside he saw a small stone chamber almost bare

of furniture. In the middle stood a round table on which incense burned, its smoke spiralling thinly upwards.

Also resting on the table were two pairs of hands.

One belonged to a thin, starved, weeping man whose shoulders shook as tears carved ravines into his tragic face.

The other hands were never still. Eight fingers and two thumbs – each shiny and sinuous as a snake – stroked the table, gripped, loosened and slithered – and then rapped it sharply.

The owner of these extraordinary hands was shrouded in a loose black robe. Only his bent head was bare and George saw waxen skin, hooded eyes and a bulbous mouth. It was from this mouth that the keening song came.

Suddenly the table replied to the knock.

It rocked violently on its legs and leaped under the four hands.

The weeping man howled like a lunatic.

'Father!' came a shout from the shadows under the window, just out of George's view. 'Please don't cry!'

George squinted down and saw Bess. She was sitting on a low bench, leaning forward with her fingers gripped into angry fists.

'Leave him alone!' she shouted at the shrouded man.

His eyes glittered and flicked a warning at her. His voice wailed.

'Beware the world of the spirit, girl. You are causing your mother great anguish. You are hurting her so much that soon she will retreat from us and in her place will come vengeful spirits to destroy you!'

'My mother has already retreated from us,' Bess cried. 'And it isn't spirits who'll destroy us, it's you! I wish you'd never come here – get out of our house!'

Solomon Sneck smiled and George could see that the sorcerer was enjoying Bess's distress. He lowered his head towards her and whispered, 'Your house, girl? Mine, I think, very soon.'

Bess flew at him with fists flying but her father stopped her. He held her close, his eyes beseeching and sorrowful.

'Be still, Daughter,' he pleaded, 'and leave us.'

'But Father—'

'Leave!' Sneck hissed, 'before I turn you into the rat you are!'

With a scream of frustration Bess fled from the house.

Bess was so upset she didn't want to see or speak to anybody. She also needed time to think what she could do about the sorcerer, and a place to think it.

So she ran into the copse behind the manor – and skidded into Big George. She had forgotten he was there.

George looked as bewildered as Bess felt.

'Did you hear that man?' she cried. 'He's going to cast a spell on me! Like he's cast a spell on my father and half the village. I hate him!'

Then, looking curiously at George, Bess added, 'You don't know what I'm saying, do you? Yet I feel that somehow you do!'

'Snool frig y nath,' George answered, smiling. 'Keep talking, I like it.' He was thinking, This girl sounds like Tilly Miller, and she *is* like her in many ways, yet she's quite different too. That was another puzzle.

Bess was thinking, This grolyhoomp sounds Welsh... though he doesn't look it. Maybe if I talk to him slowly he *will* understand me.

And so, speaking as slowly and carefully as if she was talking to an idiot, she told George about her troubles.

'My father means everybody well and thinks well of everybody,' she said, 'but Solomon Sneck means only ill. Father, because he's such a good man, can't see it. He doesn't see how strong Sneck is growing, and he doesn't understand that while he's mourning my mother, Kingswell is slipping into ruin.

'I've tried to rouse him, but he doesn't hear me because his heart is breaking. If something doesn't happen soon to shake him out of his despair, I'm afraid he might die.

'So *I* have to do something myself to stop Solomon Sneck. I don't know what, yet, but I won't let that evil enchanter kill my father, I won't!'

Bess looked defiantly at George. He smiled back encouragingly, enjoying the music of her words and the spirit flashing in her dark eyes, and winked.

That enormous slow blink was inspirational to Bess. As had happened with George himself, inside her brain a door opened and light flooded in. Astonished, she gaped at George with her eyes ballooning.

'George, I don't know how but you've just given me the best idea I've ever had. I'm going to out-magic the magician!'

An hour or so later, when Huw was shepherding his pigs through the churchyard near the grave of 'Lady Mary Griphook, Dear Lamented Wife', Sneck's hooded figure suddenly reared up in front of him.

Huw thought he'd seen a ghost and yelled. The pigs stampeded. A sow lurched into Sneck and knocked him down, and before he could get up two fat porkers trod on him while a third performed a horrid act on his face.

Horrified, Huw tried to help the sorcerer to his feet.

'Keep off me!' Sneck raged, pushing Huw away and hurriedly wiping his face on his cloak. 'If you don't keep those beasts under control I'll throw your family out of the village altogether! Think about that!'

Huw pictured his family hiding in a tree in the
frozen forest at night while wolves bayed below and
winter spirits howled in the air, and his heart sank.

Then he remembered the grolyhoomp and it rose
again.

'You don't scare me any more, Mr Almighty
Enchanter,' he muttered. 'A hero has come to
Kingswell who will flatten you if you're not careful.'

Sneck wasn't supposed to hear that, but his suspicious ears could catch a bat's sneeze five miles away and trouble ten times further.

'Hero? What hero?' he snorted. 'What a liar you are, Evans. Who'd believe anything a swineherd says?'

But as Sneck went on his way a tiny seed of doubt rooted itself in his head.

'Don't trust that boy not to be telling the truth for once,' it said. 'Keep your eyes peeled, Solomon. These are such strange times that anything could happen.'

The sorcerer looked furtively about, quickened *his* step and crossed his fingers – which goes to prove that even magicians can believe in fairies.

chapter Nine

BOY BESS

That evening the air cooled and George once again lay gathering frost, peeping into the manor – and finding another puzzle as, in the shifting light of fire and tallow lantern, he watched Bess Griphook being transformed.

Sweet-smelling herbs covered the floor of her chamber. More herbs festooned the walls. They were supposed to counter the smells of smoke and unwashed sweat but Bess paid no heed to those anyway – stinks were an everyday part of life in the Year of Our Lord 1399.

Bess had worse things on her mind.

Holding her arms up so her maid could remove her robe she asked, 'Why is it, Syb, that a girl has to become a boy to be taken seriously?'

Fat Sybil chuckled, wobbling her chins. 'Why,

child, that's just the way the world goes, innit? Men be the masters.'

'But that isn't fair.'

'Has always been so.'

'Well, that doesn't make it right. Do I keep my chemise on?'

'You'd better, child. You'll freeze without. And you shall wear a tunic over, and a super-tunic over that to keep out the cold, and also hose and a rabbit-skin hood. Everything of the coarsest stuff because you're only a poor boy seeking work.'

Bess wrinkled her nose. 'Rabbit skin! I prefer ermine and silk.'

'That's because you're a lord's daughter and live differently from the rest of us. 'Twill do you good to join the real world for a bit.'

Sybil collected Bess's new garments from a three-legged stool in a corner. A mouse sleeping under it skittered away, disturbing the hood that had once been a rabbit.

'One of these days I'll catch that mouse and pull his tail right off!' Chuckling, Sybil bustled back to Bess and began to dress her.

Sybil Stack was a jolly woman with big red cheeks, big chins and big ambitions. She saw herself not as Bess's maid but as her friend – which was true – and also as Sir Simeon's future wife, which was not.

But beneath her bluster and high hopes she was

soft-hearted, generous and utterly loyal to her young mistress.

On went the tunic, accompanied by Sybil's prattling stream of talk. 'You watch that enchanter now, girl. Don't want him enchanting you, and I wouldn't trust him as far as I could spit a goose. And as for that father of yours, a good shaking would stir him better than a spoon. Here, put a toe in this.'

Bess stared, revolted by a rag in Sybil's hand that looked more like a long-dead serpent than something to wear next to your skin. 'What is it?' she gasped.

'What's it look like? It's hose, my girl, hose!'

'It's horrible. It'll make me squirm, I know it.'

But on went the hose, slithering up Bess's legs and tickling as it went.

When the dressing was complete, down to a filthy pair of hide working boots, Bess was unrecognisable. She strutted around the chamber, scowling at the coarse cloth scratching her flesh and trying to walk like a boy.

She produced an ungainly swagger.

'Sneck won't like that,' Sybil tutted. '*He's* the swaggerer round here.'

Bess frowned. 'I'll get it right soon. I'll practise walking like Huw.'

'He drags his feet.'

'Then I'll drag my feet. I'll do anything it takes.'

She drooped and shuffled, copying the way Huw slouched after his pigs.

Watching her, a tear sprang into Sybil's eye. 'Oh, come here, child!' she cried, enfolding Bess in her ample arms. 'You're a brave girl but this is a foolish and dangerous thing you're set on. If that sorcerer sees through your disguise goodness knows what he'll do. Why, you could end up in his cauldron yourself!'

Bess shuddered. 'Don't say that, Syb. I promise I'll be careful. And now there's one last thing you must do for me.'

Sybil wiped her nose on her sleeve. 'Anything, child. What is it?'

'Cut off my hair.'

chapter Ten

The Grolyhoomp Song

Bess's transformation was a puzzle too many for Big George to take in – the last straw that broke his patience. Because it's all very well saying you will look and learn and seek and find, but when you don't understand the results it makes your head spin.

George's head was spinning all right.

He was also bored with hiding and keeping still. If you think about it, turning into an icicle must be the most boring thing in the world.

George wanted action for a change.

So he stretched his numb legs, flexed his iced-up arms and took a stiff aching step away from Griphook Manor.

And another.

George craved excitement, although if he'd

known the kind of excitement coming his way
he might not have been so keen.

But just now the very fact of moving made good
things happen inside him. Sensation returned
to his body. His feet and fingers began to
belong to him again and his blood
pumped purposefully through his veins.

With power surging through his body like
water released from a dam, George felt like
singing.

So he sang.

He sang to the moon, the stars and the hanging comet. He sang to the village and the hills.

When George sang softly he created a humming sound that reverberated inside your ears. When he let rip he produced a noise that was truly awful.

Imagine a cat's miaow, thunder and a grating door all going full pelt at once. Magnify that noise a thousand times and you're coming close to the sound of Big George singing.

Anyone out in the hills that night would have thought the world was ending.

Anyone out in the hills that night with eyes to see would also have thought they saw a gigantic pale-green lantern swinging through the mountains.

Unfortunately the only person there could not even see something as big as Big George's shining face.

His name was Biffin.

Blind Biffin.

Blind Biffin liked being out at night because he moved through darkness better than people with sight, and that pleased him. His stick was his antenna and his hearing was doubly acute – he had the sharpest ears in the Marches, sharper even than those of Solomon Sneck.

This meant that although Biffin could not see George, he heard him so clearly it sounded as if the world was being torn apart about two yards in front of him.

Biffin stopped walking.

Anxiously he waved his stick about, probing it along the frozen ground – *tap-tap*, *tap-tap*.

Blind Biffin was in his own way also a magician.

Sightless since birth, he would have liked to have been a builder and create amazing structures. Since he couldn't do that he taught himself to make amazing structures of sound – he learned music and became a magician with a harp.

Biffin's music made happy people sad and sad people happy. His tunes gave rest to the weary and peace to the tormented. They could lead you into battle and even to the grave, sending you to Heaven with a smile on your face.

People said that while Solomon Sneck's magic cured the body, Biffin's soothed the soul.

That gained him entry to every house and manor in the Marches but even so he liked the outdoors best. That was why he was here now among the borderland hills, hearing the world end.

Tap-tap, went his stick.

He took a wary step forward.

Tap-tap.

The fearful roaring noise stopped.

But the silence was worse because in it Biffin heard other sounds that were even more frightening.

He heard a footfall like a muted earthquake and breathing like a gigantic bellows.

Trembling and holding his own breath, he took another step.

Tap-tap. Tap-tap.

For months, doom-mongers had been prophesying that as the century closed unearthly monsters would appear. Biffin had scoffed then, but he believed them now.

'Th-there's a lovely monster, isn't it?' he stuttered in a lilting trembling voice. 'D-don't eat me. I'm all bones, see. Welsh bones they are, too, and they taste really horrible. You'd prefer English, look you.'

Biffin swallowed and waited for developments.

There were no developments.

There was only silence, broken by the breathing. That was slow, heavy, close and very worrying.

George had heard Biffin's stick through his singing.

Tap-tap. Tap-tap.

He had thought the hills were deserted, but at this sharp sound he shut up and stood still. He peered into the darkness ahead.

Tap-tap. Tap…

Into the range of his face glow there arrived a short bearded man wearing a long mantle of sheep's wool. The man approached George carefully, prodding a white stick.

His eyes were also white, and sightless.

The man spoke, and George thought it would be polite to reply.

'Sloop riksy friddly,' he said. 'Who are you?'

Biffin got the fright of his life.

The words reached him from an impossible height, breath blew over him like a warm wind. More than at any other time in his life he wished he could see.

He waved his stick again – *tap-tap, tap-tap* – and stepping forward jabbed it into Big George's foot.

'Oo-er,' he said.

Biffin touched George's boot with his fingers and tried to make his way round it. It took a long time – impossibly long. The boot was immensely high, too, with laces thick as hawsers.

'I don't believe this, look you,' he mumbled. 'This is a boot to terrify God.'

Biffin waited for the monster to do something.

George waited for Biffin to do something.

Neither did anything.

The weather grew colder.

And colder.

They both waited so long they froze solid and stood motionless like two icy statues on the frosty mountainside.

That is exactly what they looked like next morning when Huw the pig boy came wandering up the valley, with his pigs and half the population of Kingswell trailing behind him, looking for a missing grolyhoomp.

chapter Eleven

It's a wonder

Solomon Sneck was greedy, vain and mean. He was, in fact, the greediest, vainest and meanest man in the Marchlands and quite possibly in the whole world.

So when an odd-looking boy knocked on his door and offered to work for him for nothing but the pleasure of watching a great wizard perform wonders, Sneck's usual suspicion melted away in the warmth of adoration.

And when the boy said he came from a far distant town where Sneck's reputation was legendary, the enchanter's hooded eyes gleamed and his chest swelled with pride. So did his head.

My fame has travelled far and wide already! he thought happily. If I take on an assistant I'll be able to perform twice the magic twice as fast and my fame will travel twice as far! Or is that four times? And then taking over Kingswell will be just the beginning. There'll be no stopping me. Beetles' trotters and tail ends!

Sneck preened himself like a peacock and stared at the boy. There was something odd about him, but he couldn't put his finger on what it was. The boy's head was shaven, he looked uncomfortable in his clothes and he kept scratching – but what of that? Scratching was normal, it came with your fleas.

Sneck shook away his doubts. It's my vivid imagination, he decided. This boy is a worshipper and it's wonderful to be worshipped. Being worshipped gives you a lovely glow.

'What's your name?' he asked sharply.

The boy looked startled. 'My name?'

'You have a name?'

'Er – yes, of course. It's – ah – Richard. Yes, that's it! Dick!'

Sneck smiled indulgently, still basking in the sunshine of his long-distance fame. 'Well, Dick, if I allow you to work for me there will be four rules which you will obey as if your life depended on it – which it probably will. Do as I ask, don't get in my way, don't tell anybody my secrets – and call me sir. Understand?'

'Yes, sir.'

'Break any rule and you're toast. Clear?'

The boy grimaced. 'Clear – sir!'

'Very well. Follow me. I have a magic surgery in an hour. You can assist me.'

Sneck strode away along a bare passage.

Bess – now Richard – blinked nervously and followed. She passed doors to the left and right – all closed – behind which creatures rustled and scuttled.

At the end of the passage Sneck entered a small

room piled high with dried, wrinkled plants. He selected four and slapped them down on a table.

'Here's your first lesson. This plant is called lungwort. I use it for ailments of the chest.'

The others followed, one by one.

'Feverfew – for headaches and childbirth. Marjoram to make poultices for bruising and swellings. This last one is lemon balm, to cure fevers and colds. You got that, boy?'

'Got it,' said Bess, memorising the herbs and their uses. There seemed nothing there to cure sadness.

'Got it?' Sneck glared at her. '*Got it?*'

'Oh! Ah! Got it – sir!'

'That's better. Don't forget. Now grind them up.' He pushed a mortar and pestle across the table. 'Then grind these. And these. And these...'

As he spoke he opened cupboards and produced jars full of dried worms, toads, eels and lizards. Dozens of dead eyes stared up at Bess. She shuddered.

'Something the matter?'

'No, sir.'

'Then get on with it. I'll be back soon. Remember the four rules, if you want to live. If you don't, I'll enjoy your decease.'

Laughing at his own joke, Solomon Sneck left Bess to complete part one of her attempt to beat a sorcerer at his own game.

While Bess was learning to be a sorcerer's apprentice, Huw Evans and the villagers were trying their hardest to thaw out a frozen musician and a gigantic sign of the times.

Huw said George might be the new saviour of Kingswell and the villagers agreed.

'Were we not told there would be monsters?' they cried, chafing George's legs with their hands. 'And have we not seen the travelling star and heard rumours of wild beasts coming out of the forest to kneel down before it? Those are marvels indeed, but this – this is a true *wonder*, look you. But even wonders are useless if they are lifeless. So let us warm it up!'

George's hands were massaged, his face was slapped and his ears pulled. Children clambered over his rigid body and jumped up and down on it.

Huw pummelled the grolyhoomp's feet and the pigs snorted into his nose.

Slowly the colour of George's skin changed from blue to pink.

His fingers twitched.

When they saw this the people retreated in fright

and their children shinned down George's body like
startled monkeys.

Blind Biffin, getting the same treatment, moaned
and moved slightly.

'We're not too late!' they all cried. 'Praise the
Lord for miracles!'

They didn't know it, but the miracles had only
just begun.

Big George and Blind Biffin felt sensation
returning to their bodies and it was agony.

'Ooowwwww!' George yelled.

'Ooooohh!' screeched Biffin.

'Aaaggghhhhh!' the villagers cried in
terror, backing even further away.

Only Huw did not retreat.

He drove his pigs up close to
George – so close that the
people gasped and waited
for them to be eaten.

'George,' Huw said gently, 'you've given us a fright.'

'Grolyhoomp, Hoooooo-oo,' George whispered. ''Hal-sligrracker-bluwan-ikdedd.' (Meaning, 'I'm getting cheesed off with feeling cold!')

Watching George shivering and hearing his teeth chattering like a gigantic woodpecker drilling a tree, Huw understood.

'The grolyhoomp needs a coat,' he said. 'And a hat. And gloves. And a scarf. We'll have to make them for him.'

The villagers measured the grolyhoomp's height and girth in their minds. Then they pictured their tiny spinning wheels. The clack of their jaws dropping could be heard in Kingswell.

Like the villagers, Bess too was afraid of the task ahead.

She was afraid of forgetting a rule and becoming toast.

She was afraid of wrongly mixing a potion and poisoning somebody – though she wouldn't have minded if that person had been Solomon Sneck.

Most of all she was afraid of being recognised and having her cover broken.

She needn't have worried.

Sneck's magic surgery took place in a barn beside his house. Three fires had been lit there – not for his clients' comfort, the sorcerer was far too mean to care about that, but for effect. Thick black acrid smoke hung in the air like a pungent fog, gathering under the roof timbers and swirling about the floor. It gave the place a lurid eerie atmosphere which contributed immensely to the impression that black and powerful magic was taking place.

That smoke put the fear of the Devil into Sneck's customers, but it aided Bess by hiding her.

She stood with streaming eyes where the smoke was thickest, watching her friends and fellow villagers being fleeced by a crooked enchanter, seeing them hand over money they couldn't afford and receiving in return mumbo-jumbo and a useless poultice made from everyday herbs laced with beetles' glands and pigs' earholes.

Solomon Sneck, though, was in his element. He revelled in hocus-pocus and Bess had to give him credit for being a great showman. His performance, timed to perfection, was calculated to inspire and terrify in equal measure and to send his customers away quaking in their shoes but believing in him absolutely.

For two hours Bess watched him wheedle and bully and entrance. She saw him smear a boy's blistered tongue with – so he said – the saliva of a five-legged hare, tie the so-called intestines of an adder round the neck of an ugly girl who wanted to be pretty, and rub slugstain and nutbalm on the feet of a man with a headache.

She listened to his chants with complete bafflement, hoping that sooner or later something that made sense would turn up.

It did not.

Finally, when the surgery was over, the sweating sorcerer ordered Bess to clear up the mess.

'Those idiots believe everything I tell them,' he chortled. 'What fools they are. And Griphook is the biggest fool of all. Well, his end is near!'

He flicked an eel's head on to a fire, where it exploded in a scatter of sparks. Then he threw back his head, tossed one of his own potions down his throat, and with a rippling choking laugh that chilled his assistant's heart, fell fast asleep.

chapter Twelve

George in the Dark

By mistake Solomon Sneck drank enough potion to make him sleep for twenty four hours. For that reason he did not hear the din of the grolyhoomp's return.

But Bess did.

She ran from the barn and saw a crowd come lurching down the street, circling George like children dancing round a maypole. In front a man played a pipe and a woman whirled like a top, hysterical with excitement.

People hurried from their houses to see what was happening and join in the fun.

'So much for keeping George a secret,' Bess thought, not knowing that Huw had set up a search party to look for him. She watched George now, beaming with happiness and stepping on tiptoe to avoid crushing anyone.

'Dibdoo,' he chuntered. 'Dibdoooo!'

Everybody cheered.

There was not a man, woman or child there who did not believe that the grolyhoomp was a wonder conjured up by the spirits of this enchanted time. They fully expected others to follow, although they had to admit that this one was enough to be going on with.

'George!' Bess shouted. 'Over here!'

Having watched her turn into a boy George recognised Bess at once. He reached over the heads of the people and gathered her out of the barn door as if she weighed no more than a hayseed. Then out of the crowd he gathered Huw, wide-eyed with astonishment at the effectiveness of Bess's transformation, and held them both close to his grinning face.

'Noodlinsies,' he said happily. 'Friends.'

Looking so nearly into George's eyes, Bess and Huw felt his delight sweep through them like a wave. It was intoxicating. 'Noodlinsies,' they repeated, laughing. 'Noodlinsies!'

The word seemed a charm to ward off Solomon Sneck's evil spells.

The procession halted in the village square.

Here Blind Biffin stepped forward.

'There's work to be done,' he shouted, waving his stick for emphasis. 'Who will spin? And who will weave? Today we must work faster than we have ever worked in our lives, because before this night the Stranger must have his coat. So be off with you!'

Awed but excited by the enormity of the task ahead, the villagers hurried into their houses and began the greatest clothing exercise Kingswell had ever seen.

Years later minstrels would sing the story of this day:

'Into their houses the people ran
And the weavers wove and the spinners span
To make a coat that was not for any man.'

While in the village square three extraordinary figures – a swineherd, a giant and a girl pretending to be a boy – stood among rioting pigs and shouted 'Noodlinsies! Noodlinsies!' to each other at the tops of their voices.

The noise of George's shout shook Kingswell Manor, momentarily rousing its lord from his grief.

Shut away in the dark empty hall, Sir Simeon Griphook parted a curtain and saw a blue and green head rising above the roofs of the houses.

He blinked and looked again.

The head was still there, its mouth opening and closing like a fish.

Sir Simeon closed the curtain and sat down quickly. 'My grief is turning me mad,' he shuddered. 'I'll have to stop it.'

But stopping grieving seemed like betraying his dead wife's memory – and that sad thought made him cry all over again.

By dusk that afternoon George had his new coat – and also mittens, socks and a hood with a scarf attached that was twenty yards long and covered every inch of his giraffe neck. Since everything was made with wool shorn from the villagers' own flock George looked like a forty-foot-high Kingswell sheep.

But he felt warm for the first time since he had woken up shivering inside his hill.

Evening drew on. Big George sat in the square, thinking hard while cats rubbed against him and a little white dog with a black face lifted a leg against his boot. He took no notice.

Inside their houses the villagers were all in bed, sleeping the sound, well-deserved sleep of the exhausted.

Bess had returned to her father, who was too miserable to notice her changed appearance.

Huw was back with his family in their lowly byre.

George was alone, thinking and looking about him.

Outside the village the whale-backed hills rose blackly in the light of the rising moon. The comet hung motionless overhead, now pointing its tail at Kingswell like a bright finger.

It was very, very peaceful, and the peace entered George's heart.

He heaved a sigh. 'I should like to belong here,' he said to himself. 'Here or somewhere near. Though anywhere would do, if it would be my home.'

He thought he was learning many things. Some were to do with size, because everything here was so *small*, others with the weather, which was different each time he woke up, but most were to do with the people.

The people were like the weather, changeable. One minute they were singing, the next fighting. One moment happy and the next in tears. With them you never knew what was coming next, so it was always a puzzle.

This whole world was a puzzle when he thought about it – it seemed to George as if life on Earth must be in some sort of code, so that to understand it you needed a key to unlock the code first.

'Well,' he told himself, 'one day I may find that key. But for now I only know what I've seen and what I feel. And what I feel most of all is loneliness.'

Once more he fingered Tilly's mirror-spoon and Jo's lucky rabbit's foot, and smiling he remembered the courage of Walter of Swyre, who although only a boy had fought the greatest knights in the land for his father's sake.

Children, thought George, are the very best thing about this place. I should like to belong to the children.

That was the moment when George decided to do whatever was necessary to help Bess and Huw in their hour of need. Because somehow he felt that they needed him as much as he needed them.

'That's what noodlinsies are for,' he muttered sleepily. 'For help. Help...'

As he dozed, George's mind wandered over the things he'd seen. He wondered idly what had become of the soldiers he'd passed on his way here, but the thought drifted away from him like a feather on a breeze.

Actually, at that moment the King of England's

expeditionary force was camped in a field fifty miles away, on the edge of a frozen bog.

The King had ordered them to live off the country they passed through, but the further west they travelled the harder this became, for the weather grew steadily sharper and the people steadily poorer. By now the soldiers were half starved, behind time and very irritable.

'I'm getting a bad feeling about this expedition, Sergeant!' bellowed their Captain, a thick-necked, thick-bodied, thick-headed man called Witless who was always shouting. He was struggling to read an inaccurate map by the light of a flickering candle. 'I have no idea where we are!' he yelled. 'And the stupid yokels who live here keep directing us the wrong way!'

'I don't think they're stupid, sir,' answered his Sergeant, a stooped man with the voice and face of a sick cow and a very apt name. 'I think they do it on purpose.'

'Well, Sergeant Moo, if their purpose is to delay us they've succeeded completely. We're days behind schedule!'

That was the soldiers' worry. Big George knew nothing of it.

He was falling asleep.

chapter Thirteen

S O S

The next day two events combined to make the inhabitants of Kingswell very unhappy.

The first was that Solomon Sneck the Sorcerer discovered their grolyhoomp and took him away from them.

Sneck found the dozing George when he stumbled sleepily from his house in the early dawn in search of mouse tails and cat lice, and walked slap into George's beard in the middle of the village square. The beard did not feel like mouse tails, it felt like walking into a hedge. And even half asleep Sneck knew there wasn't a hedge in Kingswell square, unless one had sprung up in the night, which was unlikely.

He woke up at once, gaped at the monster in dismay and demanded an explanation from the villagers. When he heard the story of how this grolyhoomp had been discovered frozen in the mountains, he demanded that George be concealed immediately in the woods. His excuse was that a grolyhoomp should be a secret weapon – which, if you remember, had been Bess's idea first. There wasn't, he said, much point in having a secret weapon if your enemy could spot it a mile off.

Sneck's real reason was that having a grolyhoomp about the place could interfere with his plan to take over Kingswell. He wanted George out of the way while he found a way to get rid of him – and there was a good chance that the wolves and bears of the forest would save him the trouble.

The second event was the breathless arrival at noon of a Welsh spy, racing home to tell Owain Glyndwr that the English army was already in the Marchlands and would soon reach Wales.

For an hour the spy paused at Kingswell to refresh himself and his horse. While there he terrified the villagers with a dark tale of what was coming to them.

'Hundreds of soldiers there are, look you,' he cried, swallowing piecrust and swilling beer at the same time. 'Thousands. There's death on the march, isn't it? There's blood lust. I have seen it myself in their eyes, look you!'

He told of swordsmen, pikemen, archers and horsemen laying waste the countryside as they came. 'Looting, isn't it? Murdering. Burning. And your village is right in their path – they will walk all over you and wipe their shoes on you. Run for your lives! Run today!'

'We are not cowards,' said Blind Biffin, who was shaking nevertheless. 'Besides, where would we go? We have nowhere else.'

Before the spy resumed his journey, Solomon Sneck took him to one side.

They spoke in whispers, but Biffin was nearby and their words dripped into his sharp ears like water into a bucket.

'The soldiers are coming for Owain Glyndwr,' Sneck hissed. 'If you hand him over they'll go away.'

The spy was amazed. 'You mean *betray* our leader?'

'For money. He'd be worth a lot, wouldn't he?'

'You mean *sell* our saviour? Surrender him to certain death?'

'It's a good idea, isn't it,' Sneck purred. 'I've just had it. It would work well here too, so if you don't mind I'll keep it for myself. We'll sell *our* saviour! SOS! Holy molespit, what a wonderful, perfect plan! It will make all my dreams come true!'

When the spy went on his way Biffin told Huw and Bess what he had overheard.

'He means to sell George, doesn't he?' cried Bess. 'We must save him!'

'Isn't he big enough to save himself?' asked Biffin.

Bess and Huw were not at all sure he was. Because it seemed to them that George was a complete innocent.

chapter Fourteen

cockatrice

During the night the weather changed again. A thaw set in. Clouds covered moon, stars and comet. Fog hid the ground. Rain began to fall.

Big George, hiding in Kingswell Wood, felt the damp hardly at all, because although water dripped steadily through the bare branches above him, it slid off his oily wool coat like water from a duck's back. But it was more than a little spooky.

Mist drifted over the ground and through it the black tree trunks crowded like spectres. And that ghostly sight brought other ghosts to George's mind – ghosts of things he had seen but hardly understood.

His head was dizzy with images of horses and flags and castles and pavilions, green mountains and yellow fields, brown rivers and blue skies. His pent-up store of impressions clustered round him in the darkness like living things.

Among them he saw an untidy boy who lived with pigs, a girl who cut off her hair, a charlatan in a pointed hat who boiled newts' eye strings for a hobby, and a village clouded with anxiety.

'Have to help them,' George whispered to the night. 'But who can help me?'

The rain fell all night and ran down George's cheeks like tears.

At dawn it stopped and a weak sun peered through the clouds like an invalid poking his head out of doors.

By then the icy earth had thawed to squishy mud, the trees of the wood stood like reeds in a swamp and the people of Kingswell squelched about their houses like herons treading water.

Perhaps it was this sudden change in the weather which unbalanced Solomon Sneck, or maybe it was just his impatience. Whatever the reason, one thing is plain – this was the day the enchanter made a very big mistake.

This was the day the sorcerer grew too big for his boots.

Sneck was in a great hurry to do two things: kill the grolyhoomp and impress his new assistant –

both at the same time.

He had found that he enjoyed Richard's admiration even more than he'd expected. Adoration and praise were addictive, and he drooled with delight to see the awe in his patients' eyes when they saw his cauldron bubbling, and swelled like a balloon with satisfaction at their burbling gratitude when he presented them with a toad's gill to lash their skins at nightfall.

And to have an assistant hanging upon his words as if they were gospel was like entering paradise.

'I'll teach that boy,' he told himself smugly as he dressed that morning. 'I'll show him he's working for a god. And I'll teach that grolyhoomp a lesson he'll never forget!'

Sneck squeezed his heavy body into a tight-fitting tunic, put on his best conical hat and waited impatiently for Richard to arrive.

Bess was late, because that morning it had taken her even longer than usual to persuade her weeping father to get out of bed. So she had to run to the sorcerer's house with her coarse clothes scratching and her tom hose drooping round her ankles.

As soon as she arrived, Sneck snatched up a sack and dragged her along the passage leading to a number of rustling rooms.

At the second door he hesitated. Bess heard a frantic scuffling inside.

'Rats,' the sorcerer commented casually, 'Kingswell size.'

At the next room he stopped again, put his ear to the door and listened. There was no sound here.

Sneck ran his fingers nervously through his hair.

'Prepare to be impressed, Dick.'

Carefully he unbolted the door and slipped inside.

'Quick now – hurry, boy!'

Bess followed him in…

… and screamed. She couldn't help herself.

This room was full of bats.

They hung from beams like bunches of

grapes. They pinged desperately against a barred window. When the door opened and Bess entered they plunged at her head like a flock of starlings.

She ducked out of the way, only to find that she was crouching among frogs and toads that jumped and croaked in a whirlpool around her ankles.

She screamed again.

'Impressed, Richard, are you?' Sneck gloated. 'Well let me tell you, you haven't seen anything yet – and it will be better for you if you don't. So close your eyes. *Now!*'

Solomon Sneck had decided that the appearance of a grolyhoomp to interfere with his plans was surely the emergency when his most secret and dangerous weapon should be used.

But it *was* dangerous!

He thrust the sack at Bess, dived like a swimmer into a heap of straw in a corner and emerged clutching something that squirmed in his hand.

'Don't look, boy!' he cried, keeping his own eyes tightly shut. 'This is the one useful exotic creature that crooked necromancer sold me. Everything else I use is everyday Marchlands stuff, cunningly tweaked with spells and potions.

'But this ... this is seriously scary. It's so frightening it terrifies me! This, boy, is a cockatrice. One glance into its eyes and you're either dead or put in a trance that could last for ever. Open the sack now, Richard. *Open it!*'

Very frightened, Bess held out the sack.

Nothing happened.

She squeezed open her eyelids the smallest fraction – and wished she hadn't.

Because what she saw was Solomon Sneck stumbling around and groping for the sack with a wriggling crested snake gripped tightly in his hands.

It seemed to sense that Bess was looking and faster than lightning swung its head towards her. Its eyes, glittering with coloured lights, flashed like kaleidoscope.

They took Bess by surprise and before she could shut her own eyes tight the lights struck her.

Fortunately it was only a glancing blow diverted by her closing eyelids, but even that was like a spear piercing her brain. She staggered and would have fallen if Sneck had not thrust the creature into the sack and caught her.

'I warned you!' he snapped. 'Heed everything I

say from now on, do you hear? I told you, my word is law!'

Bess nodded dizzily.

'Now follow me, and bolt the door behind you!'

Bess stumbled out after him, feeling more than half hypnotised.

By the time they reached the grolyhoomp in the acorn wood they were caked in mud.

The sack in Sneck's hand was ominously still.

When George saw Bess he sat up and grinned.

'Bbb-ee…' he began.

She ran forward to forestall him, shouting 'Richard! I'm Richard!'

George looked surprised for a moment, but then he smiled again. These people were always playing funny games.

'Rrrr-iiiii-chchchch-aaa-rrrrr-ddddd!' he burbled.

Bess sighed with relief. 'Call me Dick,' she suggested. 'It's easier.'

Sneck shouldered between them.

'That's enough idle chat,' he snarled. 'We have work to do. Here, boy, hold this.'

He pushed the sack into his assistant's hand.

Bess gasped, feeling the cockatrice's unexpectedly heavy weight. A sudden movement almost dragged the sack from her hands. Thinking it was preparing to strike her again, she turned her head away.

Impatiently Sneck indicated to George that he was to lie down. Interested, George complied and waited to see what would happen.

What happened was an extraordinary performance as the sorcerer prepared himself for his task.

'Pay attention, boy. You're going to see a master at the height of his powers,' he boasted. 'Watch and tremble.'

Like a weightlifter girding his body for the snatch, Sneck set himself up for action.

He cracked his knuckles, flexed his arms, dipped his knees and, holding his jaw with both hands, jerked it from side to side.

His neck creaked.

To warm up he performed nineteen press-ups and twenty-six sit-ups, then attempted a high kick and fell over.

'Laugh, boy, and I'll turn you into a pancake,' he growled. 'Now give me back the sack.'

Eagerly Bess complied, although she was worried about the next bit. She watched anxiously as Sneck strode towards George, holding the sack in the air.

Furrowing his brow in concentration, the sorcerer began an incantation.

'*Hocus-pocus flummery floo*
What happens next will be the death of you.
Cockatrice eyes and cockatrice stare
Will send you to Hell and keep you there!'

His voice rose to a shriek as he whirled the sack and sent the cockatrice flying out. It writhed in the air and landed on George's chest.

Bess screamed, 'Don't look at it, George! Close your eyes!'

She was too late.

George and the cockatrice gaped at each other.

Solomon Sneck gaped too – in furious disbelief at Bess.

'Break my spell, would you, boy?' he screamed. 'You've just sentenced yourself to death!'

Sneck's arms rose. The skin tightened on his cheeks. His fingers pointed like pokers, then hooked into claws. Bess hurriedly backed away but Sneck was quicker: his claws gripped her arms ... her shoulders ... then fastened on her throat. She quailed at the murderous light in his eyes as she felt his thumbs sink savagely into the soft skin and begin to choke her.

But before Bess lost consciousness Solomon Sneck saw, out of the corner of his eye, that something unexpected was happening to his delightful pet...

When the cockatrice looked at him, George was surprised by the lights it unleashed like arrows from its eyes.

Those arrows hurt.

He didn't like that, so he blinked and bounced the arrows back like boomerangs.

Nothing like that had ever happened to the cockatrice before and it was too amazed to protect itself. Its own glance coming back sent it cross-eyed and rigid as a plank.

George picked it up.

'I think this is yours,' he said – in Halrigian, of course. Casually he dropped the cockatrice into Sneck's unprepared arms.

The fall loosened its crossed eyes and a kaleidoscopic blazing glare hit the sorcerer like a bolt of lightning.

Sneck's horrified stare turned instantly rigid. As the cockatrice flopped to the ground and slithered off into the forest, the would-be King of Kingswell slipped into a helpless trance.

An hour later Solomon Sneck was still entranced, staring at nothing with his arms raised, his fingers pointing like pokers and the skin stretched tight as a drum across his cheeks.

At his feet lay an empty sack and all around him black skeletal trees stood to attention like ghostly prison guards.

The enchanted enchanter was quite alone, because by then Bess, George and the cockatrice were long gone.

chapter Fifteen

It's a Knock-Out

Unfortunately, Solomon Sneck did not remain entranced for ever as he had threatened Bess. Sneck's cockatrice was a mere shadow of the real thing – he'd been fooled there too by the crooked necromancer. That was lucky for him, because after six hours the trance began to wear off.

By then Sneck was soaked to the skin, chilled to the marrow, sneezing continuously and angrier than he had ever been in his life.

His first thought as he emerged from oblivion was the memory of his assistant's betrayal.

His second was to vow the most spectacular revenge the Marchlands had ever seen.

His third was deciding what form that might take.

Unfortunately for Bess the sorcerer was inspired,

and the idea he dreamed up was so nasty and devious it made him laugh in the middle of his cold.

'Hatchooo!' he spluttered as he slopped into Kingswell. 'Hoosheee!' Although he was utterly filthy he didn't bother to clean himself up. He went straight to Kingswell Manor – and bumped into George in the courtyard.

George was practising how to cross your eyes on purpose to avoid the glance of a malignant cockatrice. It was part of his research.

'Just you wait,' Sneck growled as he scuttled between George's feet, 'I'll have you for breakfast.'

Some breakfast.

Without waiting to be announced the sorcerer splashed straight into the Great Hall, where he found Sir Simeon Griphook sitting at the long table with his head in his hands and his daughter crouching on a stool beside him.

Bess's buxom maid Sybil moved protectively beside them as Sneck entered.

It was lucky for Bess that she had been standing at the window watching George when Sneck entered the courtyard. She was already wearing her proper clothes and that gave her time to throw a purple snood over her shorn hair.

Sneck burst into the hall shouting with rage.

'I'll get rid of him!' he cried. 'I'll crown him in

glory then nail him to the English flag! I'll sell him for silver and the soldiers can tear him apart a piece at a time!'

Sir Simeon wailed.

Bess jumped up. 'Have you no respect?' she demanded. 'Can't you see you're upsetting my father?'

'Mind your own business,' Sneck snapped.

'My father *is* my business!'

Sybil, unable to keep silent, waded into the argument like a wrestler entering a fighting ring. She took a deep breath, which swelled her massive figure to twice its normal size. She looked terrifying.

The sorcerer was impressed.

'What are you talking about?' Sybil roared.

Sneck backed away from her. 'I've just told you!'

'We didn't understand. Tell us again slowly. And with respect, if you please.'

Slowly, grimacing with frustration but with so much apparent respect for Sir Simeon that the unhappy knight stopped weeping in amazement, Solomon Sneck explained his plan to crown his assistant Richard as Winter King at Kingswell's Midwinter Feast.

Richard, he said, would be feted and honoured, but afterwards he would be surrendered as ransom to the advancing English army in return for their promise to leave Kingswell in peace.

'I think I can guarantee English cooperation,' he added smugly.

Bess was surprised. 'How can you?'

'That's my secret.'

Sir Simeon cheered up enormously as at last he

saw a way out for his people, and his mind began to work positively for the first time in months.

'Why would the army leave us in peace?' he asked. 'King Henry wants Owain Glyndwr, not an innocent boy.'

'We'll tell them he's Glyndwr's son,' Sneck said triumphantly. 'They'll think they can catch their enemy through him!'

Bess shuddered.

'Father,' she cried beseechingly, 'don't agree!'

That was *Bess's* big mistake, because her cry clicked a switch in the enchanter's brain.

He remembered how Richard had cried out to the grolyhoomp and thought, 'That's funny. The two voices sound the same.'

He looked narrowly at Bess and mentally superimposed his assistant's face on top of it.

The fit was perfect.

Sneck gasped. 'I must have been blind!' he told himself. 'Why, the cunning little vixen! But no matter – I'll crown her Winter Queen and the soldiers can have her as Glyndwr's *daughter*!'

His mouth twitched into a smile.

'Well, Sir Simeon? What do you think of my plan?'

The knight stared at his daughter, seeing her properly at last. 'I'll think about it,' he said, 'and let you know in the morning.'

After supper Bess tossed a cloak over her shoulders and slipped out of the manor to tell Huw about Sneck's plan.

In the courtyard she looked for George but couldn't see him. She hurried across the drawbridge.

That was as far as she got.

A figure blacker than the night loomed over her. She cried out but a cloth was thrust swiftly and roughly into her mouth. Then she was bundled into a blanket, lifted up and carried away.

Huw wasn't at home anyway, he was scouring the village for a missing piglet.

It was nowhere to be found and he was turning disconsolately for home when he heard Bess's brief cry.

He ran towards the sound and was just in time to see a hooded figure carrying a bundle into Solomon Sneck's house.

Huw ran to Sneck's door and tried to open it. It was bolted.

He thumped on the heavy oak. He kicked it and shouted and the noise he made disturbed all the cats and dogs of Kingswell.

'Open up, Mr Sneck!' he yelled. 'Let me in!'

Nearby another door opened very quietly.

Footsteps crept silently.

'Let me in!' Huw shouted again.

'As you wish, boy,' whispered a gruff voice. A hand rose. Huw hardly felt the blow. And being unconscious before he hit the ground he didn't feel himself being lifted up and carried into the house of the Kingswell enchanter.

chapter Sixteen

Potion

I n the courtyard Big George was thinking, If I'm really going to help my friends I ought to *do* something. But what?

He wondered if the blind man with the tapping stick might have some ideas, and since hanging about a courtyard was as boring as becoming an icicle he set out for the hills in the hope of finding Biffin again. Besides, he liked the tapping sound of Biffin's stick, the lilt of his accent and the adventures that seemed to happen whenever they were together.

As he passed by the churchyard Huw's missing piglet came snuffling out and tagged along behind him, grunting gently.

Climbing into the mountains George watched the weather change again.

The dismal rain clouds sailed away eastward and in their wake stars pricked the sky like pins on a black pillow.

The comet, even lower and brighter than it had been before, pointed its tail directly at Kingswell.

The temperature plummeted. Soon frost was stiffening the ground again beneath George's striding feet and fingers of ice were exploring the edges of rain pools in the hollows.

The piglet, distinguished from its brothers and sisters by a black spot on its snout and a curious droop of its curly tail, trotted breathlessly at his heels.

As luck would have it Biffin was also out on the mountain, his sightless face lifted to the sky as he listened to the night.

Although Biffin couldn't hear the universe sing as George could, he had discovered that at night, when all the distracting noises of the day had been stilled, he could hear the music that *Earth* made.

He had found that Earth had its own orchestra, whose instruments were grass growing, worms turning, insects crawling, owls hooting, bats flitting – and even the ground itself expanding and contracting.

Lovely music, Biffin thought. Lovely, and very exciting.

Tonight what he heard was the sound of frost – and then of the ground shivering as if it was a drum being beaten by giant drumsticks.

Biffin knew what it was, and he was pleased. He liked the monster now and was no longer afraid of it. So he poked out his stick and set off in search of the grolyhoomp, tap-tapping his way down the mountain.

When he found George he sang, 'It is pleased I am to meet you again, George bach. Indeed to goodness, look you. Would you walk with me down to the village, please? I wish to examine you, see.'

All through that night the frost tightened its grip.

The fingers of ice crawled like spiders across the rain pools, touched and locked together.

Earth turned hard as iron.

While it did so, these things were happening.

Only twenty miles away from Kingswell the King of England's avenging army was camped in the hills and cursing the weather.

In Kingswell itself Big George lay flat in the square while Blind Biffin, trying to imagine what this monster looked like, measured him with his stick. The conclusion Biffin came to was that George was an impossibility. But that only made him more exciting.

Not far away Sarah and Rachel Evans were so worried about Huw they were hardly aware of the cold. Even so, little by little they sought comfort by moving closer and closer to the animals, finally dozing off dangerously near their hooves.

Inside Kingswell Manor, Sybil was very, very afraid for her missing young mistress. Instead of preparing Bess for bed she was lying on her cot whispering over and over like a prayer, 'Where are you, my angel? Why have you not returned to me, my lamb?'

Below Sybil, in the great hall, Sir Simeon

Griphook was gazing damply at the portrait of his departed wife and wondering about the candidate for the coronation of the Winter King in the morning.

Although he had appeared to trust the sorcerer completely Sir Simeon didn't trust him now. He felt uneasy about Sneck's proposal that his own assistant should wear the crown. There seemed a danger there, although at the moment the knight could not see where it might lie. In the end he was forced to admit that he himself could think of no suitable alternative – especially when you considered how the Winter King's short reign was going to end.

Sir Simeon marvelled at the deviousness of the plan. What a twisted mind that strange man must have!

Sir Simeon didn't know that his daughter was missing. Nobody had dared to tell him.

Meanwhile, in another part of Kingswell, Solomon Sneck was having a hilarious time concocting a new potion to send his two unwilling guests to oblivion.

As the mixture bubbled and steamed on the fire it gave off a kind of laughing gas, and every fifteen seconds Sneck roared and chuckled as he tossed in a new ingredient: fragment of tail or eyeball or sliver of sinew or poisonous toadstool.

When he judged the potion to be exactly right he scooped out a bowl of liquid stench. Then, holding it at arms' length and giggling as he went, he shuffled in flapping slippers down the corridor to the rustling rooms. At the third door he stopped, drew open the bolt and entered quickly. He saw Huw, eyes popping, pressed back against the opposite wall besieged by adders.

Sneck held out the bowl.

'Drink two sips of this,' he growled. 'No more than two, mind, or you'll be a very sick pig boy indeed.'

Huw peered at the steaming sticky lumps swimming in grease and found himself grinning. 'Why should I?' he asked suspiciously.

The magician leered. 'Because it will make you smell even worse than you do already, and the snakes will keep away from you.'

Huw risked a glance at the writhing mass at his feet and knew he had no option but to agree. Retching at the horrible smell, and in spite of grave misgivings, he took the bowl and forced himself to drink from it.

The effect was immediate: his body convulsed with laughter, then heaved, shuddered and vomited. Finally it slid helplessly down the wall to the floor.

Giggling away, Sneck left him there, and the last sounds Huw heard before he fainted away were the slamming of the bolt in the door and the soft slithering of snakes climbing over him.

Sneck entered the fourth chamber.

Here Bess stood frozen and trembling surrounded by hideous creatures. Huge rats jumped and squeaked and hissed at her with bared teeth. Deformed spiders humped about the floor. Wingless bats flopped in corners.

There was ceaseless movement everywhere with Bess rigid in the middle like the still eye at the centre of a hurricane.

She was so frightened she would do anything to keep these revolting creatures at bay and when Sneck offered the promising bowl she drank from it so quickly she gagged as she giggled. Purple slime dribbled down her chin.

The enchanter was only half way through the door when Bess followed Huw's lead and sank glassy-eyed to the floor.

Rubbing his hands with satisfied glee, Solomon Sneck returned to his kitchen knowing that his prisoners would be out of action for a very long time.

Too long, as it turned out.

chapter Seventeen

who will Be crowned?

The next day was Christmas Eve – that eager, anxious time when the world seems to be holding its breath in anticipation of a great wonder to come.

It was certainly a breathless time in Kingswell, because very early in the morning four important things with far-reaching effects happened in as many minutes.

First: a small grey insignificant-seeming cloud wandered out of the west. When it reached Kingswell it paused and hung and loosed a few spinning flakes of snow.

Second: Sarah Evans, so heavy with child she could hardly walk, visited the sorcerer's house to ask for a spell to help find her missing son. She knocked on Sneck's outer door just as, in the courtyard, the sorcerer was shoving his assistant Richard – 'who had unfortunately fallen and bumped his head', said Sneck – on to a decorated cart in readiness for the parade of the Winter King.

The magician peered through the door, listened impatiently and sent Sarah packing. 'Go into the forest,' he snapped, 'and look for wild pigs. Your son will be the ugliest among them.'

Third: As Sarah Evans turned disconsolately away a pair of hefty unpleasant-looking bruisers pushed past her with an unpleasant scowl. Solomon Sneck, who'd met them during a recruiting mission in the dark alleys of Shrewsbury, was expecting them. Looking furtively about him he beckoned them inside and closed the door quickly.

In the courtyard he looked them up and down and grinned. 'Scalding bluebottles,' he chortled, 'I chose well. You look as likely a pair of villains as ever put the frights up innocent citizens. You're just what I want. I hope you and your cronies are handy with your fists, for you're going to help me conquer Kingswell!'

Fourth: As if by magic Sir Simeon Griphook, Lord of the Manor of Kingswell, changed back from the weeping mouse he'd become to the gentle, kindly, brave knight he once had been.

He woke early, still pondering the choice of

Winter King, and found to his surprise that this morning the overwhelming sadness he had experienced at the loss of his dear wife felt just a little less unbearable now he had something else to worry about.

He left his bed, padded to the window, drew back the curtains and saw two things: a snowflake and a grolyhoomp.

The first he ignored; the second changed everything.

Dashing through his manor shouting, 'The King! The King! I've found the King!' Sir Simeon flew into the courtyard and gazed rapturously up at the most shocking and wonderful being he had ever seen – who just at that moment was trying to catch snowflakes for educational purposes.

Awed by Big George's size, neck, colour – by everything about him – the knight bowed and said, 'Sir, I honour you. You're a wonder and no mistake.'

George bowed back. 'Grolyhoomp,' he said.

'And the same to you.'

Blind Biffin came tapping across the drawbridge. 'That's a grolyhoomp, look you, sir,' he said.

'Ah,' Sir Simeon said wisely. 'A grolyhoomp, eh? Well of course that explains everything.'

Behind Biffin the population of Kingswell

streamed over the drawbridge, dressed in their very best finery for the Midwinter Feast and the Coronation of the Winter King.

Noisy and excited, they crowded into the courtyard around Big George, who beamed down at them and said, 'Can I belong here?

That was his second time of asking, and once again the people did not understand him.

But it seemed as if they did, because what happened next appeared to George to be the biggest vote of confidence he could imagine. Sir Simeon Griphook bowed low before him and then – smiling for the first time in months – turned to his people and said, 'Behold your Hero, your Spirit of Christmas, your Winter King!'

The villagers went wild, because this was exactly what they themselves had been hoping for ever since the moment when they first saw this amazing wonder frozen on a mountainside, and thawed him out and made him the clothes that had warmed him ever since.

They jumped for joy, and cheered.

They patted George on his legs and boots – the only bits of him they could reach.

They praised Sir Simeon for having such a wonderful idea – and for stopping crying.

A squinting friend of Biffin's handed him his

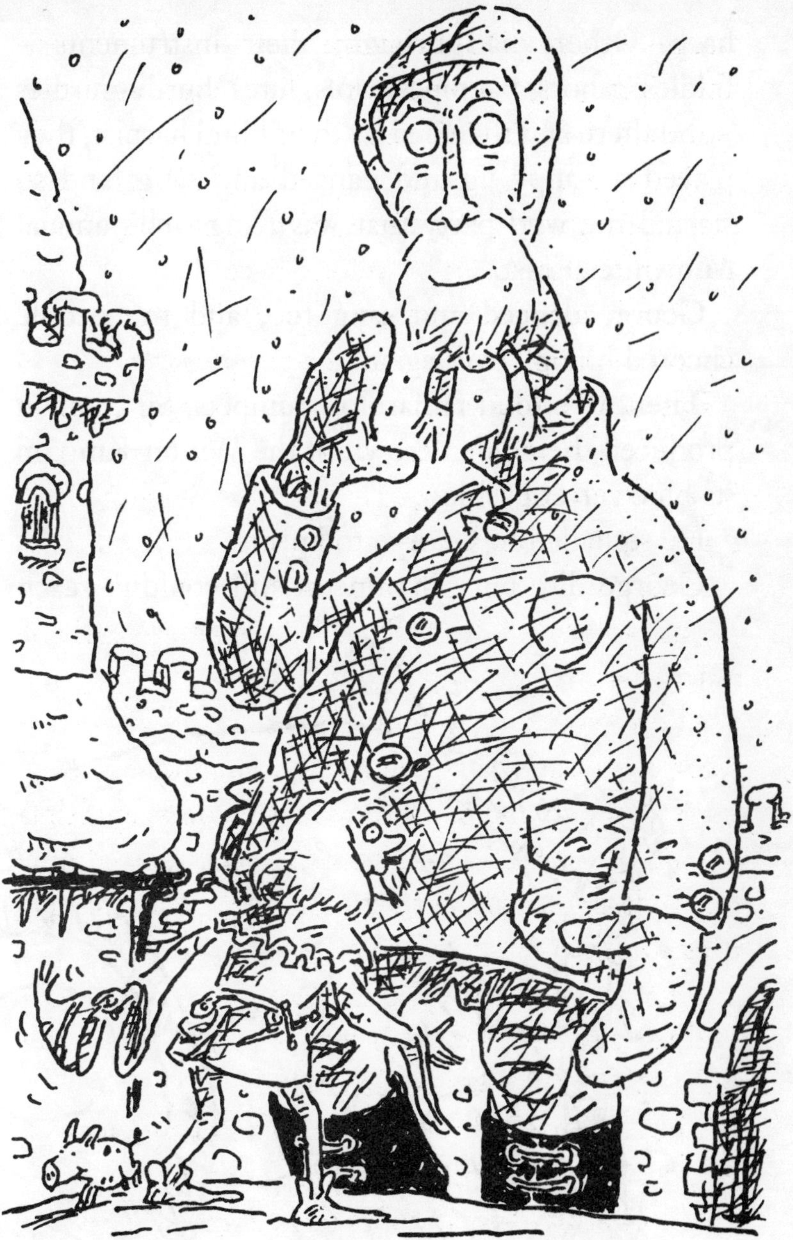

harp. Others had brought their instruments – fiddles, tabors, bagpipes, viols, lutes, hurdy-gurdies – and there and then, led by their blind harpist, they played a happy jig and danced and sang, and so started the wild party that was Kingswell's annual Midwinter Feast.

George danced and sang too, and the people cheered him all over again.

Then, to a loud fanfare of trumpets, Sir Simeon produced the golden crown of the Winter King on its blue velvet cushion.

He signalled to George to kneel.

George did, but Sir Simeon still couldn't reach

his head. So he asked George to lie down.

George lay down to please him, and Sir Simeon Griphook, Lord of the Manor of Kingswell in the Marchlands of England and Wales, stepped solemnly forward, and with the words 'I crown thee Spirit, Lord and Winter King!' set the golden crown into George's blue and green wiry hair.

Next the village priest, a tiny man with elfin ears and a dreamy look, was lifted up so he could sprinkle George with holy water. 'I baptise you Holy Fool,' he piped. 'May the Spirit of Christmas be with you and bless your reign with good things!'

George rose to his feet feeling pleased and happy without knowing why. As if echoing this uncertainty, his crown slipped sideways. But it stayed on his head.

'Long live the King!' the people shouted. 'Long live the Winter King!'

*

If you're wondering, 'Have the people of Kingswell gone mad? Have they forgotten that a vengeful army is bearing down on them?' the answer is – well, no, they haven't.

But since that prospect is too frightening to think

about, they have decided not to think about it. With a bit of luck, they're telling themselves, it might not even happen – why, those soldiers could march by on the other side of the mountain and not even realise that Kingswell is here!

Hope springs eternal.

Besides, very little in this world is absolutely perfect. You can find a flaw in most things if you look hard enough.

For Big George the flaw in his great celebration appeared when he looked for Bess and Huw to share his happiness and couldn't find them. Puzzled, he looked over the heads of his dancing subjects and called, 'Hoo-oo-oo! Bbeee-ssss!'

Everybody thought he was singing – except Sir Simeon Griphook. 'Bess?' he exclaimed. 'Yes, where is she? Where's my daughter! *Bring me my daughter!*'

In that heart-stopping moment the knight had found *his* flaw.

Sybil was brought before him, weeping for her lamb and wailing that it wasn't her fault she was missing.

'Missing?' cried Sir Simeon. 'Bess is MISSING?!'

Begging Fate not to be so cruel as to deprive him of *both* the creatures he loved most in the world, Sir Simeon ran into the manor and began to search it inch my inch. His desperate voice could be heard calling for his daughter even through the tumult of instruments and flying feet in the courtyard.

And now it was time for the people of Kingswell to find the flaw in *their* happiness.

It came rolling over the drawbridge towards them in the shape of a cart driven by two terrifying toughs. On the cart Solomon Sneck sat in his best sorcerer's suit with his arm propping up a sleeping youth who was so heavily cloaked and hooded as to be unrecognisable.

A cardboard crown trembled on the youth's head.

The Kingswell sorcerer was absolutely furious – more furious than he had ever been before in his furious life.

He was furious with the people of Kingswell for starting the festivities without him.

He was furious with Bess for making him late, and as they crossed the drawbridge he slapped her cheeks for the twentieth time and hissed, 'Come to, girl! Come to!', cursing her blank eyes and lolling face and the sleeping potion into which he'd clearly tossed too many thrushes' eye linings.

He was furious with the grolyhoomp for wearing the crown of the Winter King – how *dare* he? – and he was furious with that ninny Griphook for giving it to him.

Solomon Sneck was furious with everybody in the world except himself.

And now that his plan to install Bess as Winter King had been foiled, the presence of his knocked-out assistant was an embarrassment.

'Take the cart back to the house,' he hissed to his gap-toothed bully boys. 'Put this dozy object back where it came from and return quickly. It's time for us to make our move.'

Then, smiling a ghastly smile that looked as genuine as a pantomime horse, the magician jumped down from the cart and joined in the dancing with a clumsy skip.

Sneck's leer would have been even less genuine if he'd known his command had been overheard.

Once again the needle-sharp ears of Kingswell's blind harpist had pierced a private conversation.

Laying down his harp Biffin collected his stick from Squinter and followed the sound of the cart out of the courtyard.

Chapter Eighteen

King For a Day or Two

Big George gazed in wonder at the strange things happening around him.

He saw more snow clouds sweeping in overhead, each heavier than the one before and loosing flakes that steadily grew bigger and fell faster.

He stored up impressions, looking, listening, learning, and saw the courtyard, the manor and even the people turning white before his eyes. He watched the world being transformed.

Looking up he saw millions of falling slivers of ice. Dozens of them stabbed his eyes and made him shiver.

He looked down and saw that the flakes were covering his mittens, knitting a white overmantle on his coat – and blanketing the bewildered snout of the oinking little piglet at his feet.

George picked it up and tucked it into his pocket, from where its two wide wondering eyes gazed curiously up at him.

Suddenly he became aware of another pair of eyes watching him. Beady, suspicious, piggier than a real pig's could ever be, they glared at him out of the snouty face of Solomon Sneck, sending out signals of pure hatred.

George instinctively understood. 'The sorcerer is my enemy,' he told himself. 'I'll have to watch him.'

He couldn't watch for long because suddenly the people, carried away by their excitement, grabbed hold of him, pulled him over the drawbridge and began the Parade of the Winter King through the streets of Kingswell.

Trumpeters blared one fanfare after another. All around George the villagers danced. The children clutched his legs and every dog and cat for miles ran squabbling behind.

'*Honour the Spirit of Christmas, look you!*' Squinter shouted, tossing Biffin's harp into the air like a flag.

'We honour him!' the people answered.

When they had circled the village twice they returned to the drawbridge. As they approached, George saw Sneck talking conspiratorially with the ruffians, who had brought along a dozen more thugs as ugly as themselves. They looked like a villainous private army.

When he saw the parade returning, Sneck ushered them all into the manor.

Across the drawbridge, through the courtyard and into the great hall the musicians, dancers, children, dogs and cats flowed – all with mouths watering at the prospect of the feast to come.

Everybody, that is, except one.

Big George could not get through the door and was left outside.

George was alone again.

Alone alone alone alone – he was always alone.

Yet this time not quite alone. The piglet in his pocket looked up at him and twitched its snout in a friendly fashion.

'Oink,' it said.

Then George saw Biffin approaching.

Tafth-tafth, *tafth-tafth* went his stick as it snuffled through the thickening snow. It stopped when it struck George's boot.

'That you, George bach?'

'Grolyhoomp,' said George.

'Oh, George, happy I am to find you. Come this way if you will, will you?'

The blind man tafthed away again, and George followed.

As they walked through the village George marvelled at the speedy transformation of Kingswell.

Already it was whiter than Biffin's eyes – the houses were festooned with whiteness, the mountains reared white all around – the very air was white with falling snowflakes. Everywhere George looked was dazzling.

This had an odd and unexpected effect. It pushed that door in his mind a fraction wider and lit up a scene in his damaged memory.

He remembered a landscape, also white, although its whiteness was not caused by snow but by sand and glittering quartz and pale, stricken stones that stretched away for ever in a limitless blinding desert.

Scattered about the desert were cities even more dazzling, great bubbles of glass, maybe, or shining metal – colossal at any rate – and dazzling because the glass reflected back the dangerous rays of a frozen, faraway sun.

In the whirling snow George paused and tried to look into the cities but Biffin snapped him back to Earth.

'Concentrate, George, please! Huw and Bess need you. Look at the house in front of you.'

Biffin too was looking through his memory – the

memories of a blind lifetime in Kingswell where every house and tree had become familiar to him through touch and smell and sound and echo. Now he pointed his stick at Solomon Sneck's barn.

George blinked, the glass cities vanished and the snow stung his eyelids.

'What I'd like you to do, George,' Biffin said, 'is demolish that building. Knock it flat. Can you do that?'

He kicked out a foot to show what he meant.

George understood.

He walked forward, measured the distance, drew back his boot and rammed it into the barn. Three of its four walls fell down.

Out of the dust snakes slithered, bats soared, spiders scuttled – and Huw and Bess stumbled like drunken ghosts.

'Hooo-ooo-ooo!' George shouted happily. 'Bbb-eee-ssss!'

They seemed to be having difficulty grasping what was going on – a feeling George knew very well – so he scooped them up and dropped them into his pocket beside the mirror-spoon, the rabbit's paw and Huw's long-lost piglet.

chapter Nineteen

Sir Solomon

Inside Kingswell Manor Solomon Sneck was making his bid for glory. Protected by his private army he burst without warning into Sir Simeon's personal chamber, surprised the lord at his desk, astonished Sybil who was making up the fire, arrested them both and locked them in the attic.

Then he marched into the great hall and announced to the feasting throng that their previous lord was a prisoner and he, Solomon Sneck, was the new owner of Kingswell Manor and their rightful lord and master.

He was, he said, to be addressed from now on as *Sir* Solomon. If anybody had any objections they were welcome to join sobbing Simeon in the attic and, when the King's army arrived, on the scaffold as well.

Nobody objected.

With their eyes popping, their mouths ajar and their fingers dripping gravy, the villagers could only gape in astonishment.

'You may show your appreciation of this great news,' said Sir Solomon, 'in the usual way.'

Imagining the spells and blows that would rain down on them if they disobeyed, his new subjects cheered and clapped and sang 'For he's a jolly good fellow' as if they had just heard the most wonderful tidings in history.

So when Big George returned to the manor he found that the world had changed again.

He was no longer the centre of attention. Far from it – as he put Bess and Huw gently down in the courtyard snow he saw the villagers prancing out of the manor chairing Solomon Sneck on their shoulders and singing praises to *him* instead.

They would have ignored George entirely if Sneck, his eyes burning with hatred, had not shouted, 'Arrest those three! And give me that crown!'

The procession stopped in its tracks. The people looked uncomfortably at each other.

'Well? Why don't *you* do it?' Sneck asked the ruffians whose looming presence had lent authority to his takeover. 'Get on with it!'

But while they had felt very big and brave in front of a bunch of helpless yokels, those toughs didn't feel half as tough in front of Big George. They felt jumpy as grasshoppers.

They looked at George and winced and asked themselves questions like, 'How can we arrest *that*? How can we take the crown off it? How do we reach it? We'll have to climb up it!'

Warily they moved forward.

What happened next was entirely unexpected, especially by Sir Solomon Sneck.

Bess and Huw positioned themselves between his bully boys and George.

'Go away,' said Huw.

'Go back in your holes,' said Bess. 'You ought to be ashamed of yourselves.'

Solomon Sneck lost all patience. Turning to his new subjects he screamed, 'DO SOMETHING!'

That was the moment when everything *really* went wrong for Bess and Huw. Scared silly by the sorcerer the crowd turned into an angry mob and surrounded them. Biffin was knocked down in the rush. 'There's bad manners!' he cried. 'What is going on, look you? This is rebellion against our true lord and rightful Winter King!'

Nobody listened to him.

Huw tried to pull Bess through the crowd. 'Come on,' he said grimly, 'We'll hide in the forest!'

But, as if a spell had truly been cast over them, the people who had once been their friends closed in.

'Leave us alone!' Huw shouted, butting a fat man's billowing stomach. The man grunted and lifted him off the ground by his collar. 'Gotcha!' he cried.

Then a woman with a broken nose elbowed Bess in the face as if she was trying to break her nose too. Bess saw stars and collapsed into the woman's waiting arms.

What was Big George doing while all this was going on? He was watching the world ending. Snow was suffocating it. What had been a breeze when the fall began had stiffened into a gale which hurled the snow like sling shot against his cheeks and eyes. It whipped up drifts and piled those drifts like barricades against buildings, trees and mountains alike.

There was nothing about this snow that was beautiful any more. It had become a wild thing, more dangerous and frightening than any animal, and Kingswell was foundering beneath its assault like a ship sinking into unknown depths of ocean.

Suddenly the gale doubled in ferocity. Anyone small or frail buckled at once beneath its force.

A girl, blown to her knees, tried vainly to tear the matting snow from her hair and eyes. 'We're going to die!' she sobbed. 'The storm will kill us!'

'Get back inside the manor!' Solomon Sneck commanded, wanting to be there himself. 'Bring the prisoners!'

Shielding their raw and bleeding faces as best they could, the villagers dragged Bess and Huw inside.

'George, we need you!' cried Bess, as the door closed behind her.

'Grolyhoomp!' Huw shouted, 'Help us!'

But George wasn't listening.

The manor door was bolted fast against the storm. The courtyard was abandoned except by the howling wind, the blistering snow and an awesome snowman who was big in every way and getting bigger by the minute.

Suddenly, for an extraordinary split-second, the clouds parted to reveal a star bright as the sun pointing down at the snowman and haloing his head with its light. It lasted only a moment, then the clouds merged again, the star vanished and the snow fell even faster than before.

Everything seemed the same, but, as if that light had been a signal, the snowman shook the snow from his head and strode out of the courtyard.

chapter Twenty

Reunion

Luckily there was one bright silver lining to the dark clouds pressing in on Kingswell that eventful Christmas Eve.

When Bess and Huw were thrust into the attic, what celebrations there were!

'Daughter,' Sir Simeon croaked, his eyes spouting like fountains, 'is that you? Is that really you?'

'Of course it is, Father!' Bess leaped into his arms. 'Though I'd be dead if your precious magician had his way!'

'I'll throw him in gaol!' Sir Simeon cried. 'I'll have him executed at once!'

'How can you? He's taken over the village.'

'He may think he has,' said Sir Simeon bravely, drawing himself up very tall and straight, 'but he has me to deal with first.'

The knight looked magnificent in his anger and Bess, who had quite forgotten how noble her father could be, felt tears surge into her eyes too. 'Oh, Father,' she sobbed, hugging him tight, 'you've come back to us!'

Sir Simeon frowned. 'When I thought I had lost you, child, I realised that one shouldn't mourn the dead at the expense of the living. I'm ashamed of myself.'

Sybil was also weeping tears of happiness. Crying, 'Lamb! My lambkin!' she bustled out of the shadowy eaves and clasped Bess to her billowy bosom. 'Dear girl, promise you'll never leave me again – I couldn't bear it!'

All was rapture.

Huw, hovering awkwardly in the shadows like the humble pig boy he was, smiled at their happiness and longed to be with his own family.

He wondered if he had a new brother or sister yet. How they needed him, he thought. But now here was Sir Simeon Griphook holding out his hand, beckoning him.

'Come here, boy,' the knight said. 'Have you been leading my daughter astray?'

Huw swallowed. 'No sir, I have not.'

Bess hurried to his side. 'No more he has, father,' she said stoutly. 'If anything it's the other way round. Huw is my friend.'

Sir Simeon's eyebrows rose. 'A swineherd dares to call himself my daughter's friend?'

'What does it matter what he is?'

The knight shook his head and smiled. 'It matters nothing, my dear child. Except that if Huw is your friend, then he's mine too.'

'And mine!' Sybil cried, embracing Huw like a friendly python.

'Give me your hand, boy,' said Sir Simeon.

And so it was that a lowly swineherd shook hands with a lord of the manor and was kissed by his daughter and her maid, and all four laughed as though they had quite forgotten that they were prisoners awaiting execution the moment the King of England's army should arrive.

chapter Twenty-one

George in Danger

Not half a dozen miles away, that army was in a sorry state. Its horsemen were no longer horsemen because their horses, having had quite enough of this fools' errand, had bolted during the night. So all Christmas Eve a miserable troop of exhausted foot soldiers – starving, soaking, freezing and weighed down by armour and weapons – struggled on foot through a snowy whiteout and drifts as high as their heads.

When they could struggle no more, they mutinied. They threw down their weapons, sat in the snow and refused to march a step further.

'I'll have you horse-whipped for this, you naughty men!' Captain Witless cried.

'Makes no difference,' the mutineers replied dully. 'We'll all be stiffs by tomorrow. We're going to die in this Godforsaken wilderness on Christmas Day!'

The Captain laid his head in his hands and prayed, harder than he had ever prayed in his life. Because he too believed that they were going to perish in the snowstorm, he prayed deep in his heart for help, even though he knew that in this alien country and unearthly weather there was no help to be had.

How wrong he was…

That small desperate cry from a desperately small soldier sent vibrations through the air which, in their own small way, were very powerful.

The Captain's prayer climbed the white windy mountains, slid down the snow-clogged valleys and slipped into Kingswell and Big George's ears at the very moment when Bess and Huw were being overwhelmed by the turncoat villagers.

It was that prayer which had distracted George from helping them. It was still distracting him when through that hole in the storm the comet momentarily reappeared and pointed – so it seemed to George – to the other side of the mountain.

It was a message which could not be ignored, so once again a grolyhoomp set out to follow a star.

Inside Kingswell Manor the Midwinter Feast was turning out to be like no other in the village's history.

Snow smothered the windows and darkened the hall. The villagers watched themselves being buried and completely lost their appetite for feasting and dancing.

Nor was Solomon Sneck as happy as he had expected to be, because already he was discovering what all rulers discover – that power is no picnic. All it does is bring responsibility.

The people of Kingswell lost no time letting their new lord know that he was responsible for them – for their present, their future and their very lives.

Questions stabbed Sneck from all sides.

'What will we do, sir, when the soldiers come?'

The sorcerer sneered. 'That's easy. Give them the fools in the attic.'

'But what if that doesn't satisfy them?'

'Give them the grolyhoomp.'

'Who's going to do that, sir?'

Sneck pointed to his henchmen, who backed hastily away.

'Don't look at us,' they said. 'Don't ask us to do anything with anybody tall. We've got no head for heights.'

The people's demands grew more and more
outrageous.

'What if this snow doesn't stop, sir?'

'It will stop.'

'But what if it doesn't? Will you make it stop?'

'How can I prevent snow from falling?' cried
Solomon Sneck, beginning to feel like a cornered
animal.

'You're a sorcerer, aren't you?'

*'You **say** you're a sorcerer. So prove it. Make the snow
stop now.'*

'Yes, now.'

'Do it NOW!'

Despairing, the sorcerer watched the people
becoming an unruly mob again. He saw their faces
turn ugly with fear, heard their voices whine like

summer flies about the winter hall, and began to hate them.

'Why did I ever want to have anything to do with these peasants?' he wondered. 'Have I made another big mistake?'

Four miles away, Big George had made a very big mistake. He'd got lost.

George was used to being lost because he'd been lost ever since he landed on Earth, but this was different.

What worried him now was that he was as blind as Biffin. He could see nothing. His eyes were clogged with snow. So were his ears. He was alone in a blanked-out, whited-out, furiously swirling world. Twice he stumbled into drifts and almost fell.

The most worrying thing, though, was that with every passing snowblind moment the prayer he was supposed to be answering was getting weaker.

Then suddenly and unexpectedly another cry, coming from the opposite direction, clanged in his mind like an alarm bell. 'Save me!' it shouted.

George recognised Huw's voice.

What could have happened to *him*?

chapter Twenty-Two
One Good Turn

Huw Evans had done a very foolish thing. Imprisoned in the attic he had been growing frantic to know how his family was faring in this most terrible of snowstorms. Was Rachel safe? Was his mother well, or ill? Did they have food, and a fire?

The questions whirled in his head and made him so dizzy that in the end he couldn't help himself. Without telling Sir Simeon, Sybil or even Bess what he intended to do, he waited until their backs were turned – and committed suicide.

Well, not quite, but he might have if it had not been for the snow.

He squeezed through a tiny attic window and slid down the roof above the kitchens to the battlements below. It was only snowdrifts slowing him down which prevented him rolling over the battlements into space.

The snow helped him in another way too. Because of it there were no guards on the battlements to see him. Everybody was in the great hall.

So, quicker and lighter than a wraith Huw slipped past drifted-up windows and down almost blocked stairways until he reached the ground.

There was a heart-stopping moment when he thought he heard Bess calling him, but the howling wind drowned it and all other sounds. Soon he was forging across the snowy courtyard and over the

almost vanished drawbridge to safety.

Or so he thought.

But Huw wasn't safe at all.

The storm's power astonished and frightened him. Beyond the drawbridge he turned towards his home but became confused almost at once. There were no landmarks any more, only wind-worried flakes that whipped and slashed his face. Everything was moving – falling, rising, spinning crazily.

The result was that when Huw thought he was approaching the cowshed he was actually following Big George out of the village.

Quickly his hands, feet, face and legs lost all feeling.

Soon he found he could not move at all.

He sank to his knees in the snow.

Hot tears melted the ice on his cheeks as he cried out, 'Mother! Rachel! Where are you!'

Slowly, like an axed tree, he toppled forward.

When his face hit the snow his mind was still searching frantically for inspiration. He had almost lost consciousness when it came.

'Grolyhoomp!' he cried, 'Save me!'

That put George in a terrible quandary.

'Help!' came the fading cry from in front of him.

'Help!' drifted Huw's weak cry from behind.

Even Big George could not travel in opposite directions at the same time. One must be sacrificed. But which one?

George knew that if he continued to plunge forward he might be able to rescue the stranger. On the other hand, if he turned back he might save a friend.

Which would *you* choose?

George didn't hesitate. He wiped the snow from his face, brushed it off his clothes and gazed at the white, blank, spinning world all around. Then he smiled. There was no contest.

He turned around and went back for his friend.

*

Huw, slipping towards death, dreamed of babies, cows and lost piglets. He was so far gone he did not see George loom out of the blizzard and gather him up as if *he* was a baby. Nor did he feel George's breath warm his face and body.

Huw did not realise that, just as a few days earlier he had helped save a gigantic stranger from an icy end, so now that stranger was saving him.

All he was aware of – and this too seemed like an extraordinary dream – was that one moment he was suffocating in snow and the next a distant owl was calling 'Hooo-oo-oo, hoooo-oo-oo!' Then he was falling into a dark comfortable shelter and landing on something soft and warm and noisy.

'Oink oink!'

'Oink!' it squealed.

As Big George turned round again, inside his pocket the piglet snuffled Huw's face with its hot little snout and began to revive him.

Chapter Twenty-Three

Action Grolyhoomp

Outside the door to the attic the first of the sorcerer's no longer brave henchmen hesitated. (Their colleagues, frightened by the storm, had fled while they could. These two heroes had stayed because they had nowhere else to go.) Each carried a platter of gruel for the prisoners.

They paused because, if there was one monster in Kingswell might there not be two? And might not the other one be in the attic, just waiting to pounce?

Bracing themselves and ready to run for their lives, they unbolted the door and faced the unknown together.

What faced them was a girl.

'Food for you,' they said, trembling with relief.

'You ought to be ashamed of yourselves,' the girl said.

The ruffians peered over Bess's head and sniffed. They could smell no monsters, They were safe. They became brave again.

In the shadows they saw Sir Simeon Griphook sitting on the floor and Sybil lovingly and hopefully combing his hair.

'Where's the other one?' they growled.

'What other one?' said Bess innocently.

'The boy.'

'Oh, him. He's gone.'

'*Gone*?' Their podgy fingers shook. 'What d'you mean, he's gone?'

'He escaped when you came in. That's what we'll say anyway.'

'Oh my. Oh my!' Pushing the platters into Bess's hands the ruffians bolted the door and tumbled down the stone staircase.

'We never heard that, right?' they panted. 'We never heard that at all. And now we're getting out of here.'

That's what they thought, but they weren't going anywhere. The snow wouldn't let them.

And what was George doing? George was getting excited. Action suited him. He was having an adventure and doing something useful at the same time and he didn't feel lonely any more.

Listening keenly for that ever-weakening signal, he forged through the driving flakes. Every minute he had to kick snow off his boots, spit it from his mouth and squeeze it out of his eyes.

Then he realised that the cry for help had stopped.

George pushed harder. His boots crunched and his breath rasped in the cold air.

He stopped to listen again.

No prayer.

No anything.

He was too late.

Then very faintly, so faint it was hardly more than a disturbance in the air, he heard a quite different sound. It seemed to come from somewhere just ahead.

Dat. Dat. Da-dat.

George had heard that noise once before, on his way here. It was the sound of a beating drum.

The drummer was a very young and very small soldier called William Tagg.

Sitting in the snow watching more snow covering his legs, William knew he was going to die because his companions had told him so. He looked round at them – little scattered humps like white bags in the snow. They had given up all hope.

But there was a difference between William and

them: he didn't know how to give up. Even now, with almost his last breath, a tiny flicker of purpose flared in him.

William was a drummer. Drumming was what he was trained to do. It was his reason for living. He couldn't stop.

So now, slowly and achingly, with the last spark of his energy he drummed. His hand lifted the drumstick and let it fall against the stretched hide.

Dat.

And again.

Dat, Very softly. *Dat.*

Hardly knowing what he was doing, William repeated the action like an automaton.

Dat. Dat. Dat.

Slowly his head slumped on to his chest. His eyes closed.

Now even William Tagg could do no more.

But what he had done was enough.

When he summoned his last remaining strength to open his eyes, he saw a monster ploughing through the snow towards him.

The thing approached, pushing through a swirling curtain of snow flakes and looking much as William had imagined a mammoth might look.

William sighed. His arm, acting entirely by itself, flipped.

Dat dat!

The mammoth towered over William, looked down, grimaced – and spoke.

'Grolyhoomp,' it said.

'Same to you,' William whispered – and passed out.

chapter Twenty-Four

George Gets Mad

Christmas Eve drew on, blind as a mole in the storm. By afternoon what daylight had escaped the hanging snow clouds was fading fast inside the manor.

Torches were lit, and in the great hall their smoky light illuminated a nightmare scene.

Dogs, clearing the floor of scraps, squabbled over crumbs.

Blind Biffin tapped anxiously among them, worrying about Sir Simeon and Sybil and Bess and Huw – and even more about Big George, lost out there in the snow.

The old minstrel tried to chant the story of the Winter King all over again, but he was howled down by the people who, hungry and afraid, gnawed greedily at the remains of the morning feast. Their mouths slopped beer and their fists fought over pieces of piecrust and gristle from the trenchers.

Several of the more pious villagers knelt in corners with their hands pressed tightly together, faces raised, eyes closed and lips mumbling.

Others continued to harangue their new lord, demanding protection from every possible misfortune with which fate might attack them. Solomon Sneck regarded them all with scorn.

'Keep those fools away from me,' he commanded his henchmen who, as much as Bess and Sybil and Sir Simeon were imprisoned by the storm.

They were annoyed about that and fed up with the sorcerer.

'You're joking,' they said. 'There are scores of them and only two of us left. How do you suggest we do it?'

'Use your initiative!' Sneck snarled. 'Do I have to tell you how to do everything?'

'Not everything absolutely, Squire. But you might show some respect.'

'Respect!' Sneck roared with laughter and slapped his legs at the joke. '*I* respect villains like *you*? I respect a sheep's backside more than you!'

'Do you really?' they said. 'Well, well.'

They closed in on him and the sorcerer, eyeing the baying villagers below him and the mutineers in front, suddenly felt a little less secure.

'I'll put a spell on you!' he hissed.

'Try it.'

'Very well, I will!'

The enchanter raised his arms like a conductor and, staring them in the eye, intoned in his deepest, most ominous voice:

Hex, hex, toadlings two
Do whatever I tell you to do
When I snap my fingers
When I show you my hand
You will obey my every command!

He snapped his fingers and slapped each ruffian across the cheek. 'There,' he said triumphantly, 'now try to disobey me.'

They grinned. 'D'you want us to do it together or one at a time?'

'You incompetent ninnies,' the sorcerer screamed, 'you're so stupid you can't recognise a spell when it hits you in the face! Why, you're the thickest—'

The tips of two swords pricked his throat.

By now the only light in the courtyard was slanting down from the flaring window of the great hall and up from the pale, ghostly, luminous snow.

The snow was still falling relentlessly, deep enough now to reach a man's shoulder.

Solomon Sneck, with those swords threatening his throat, looked through the window for salvation – and gasped.

Something very strange was happening out there. An enormous tree branch pushed forward through the gateway and cleared it like a snowplough. Then it moved into the courtyard, sweeping left, right, left, right, powering away the drifts and making a passage through.

Into that passage there staggered a small figure whose arms rose and fell like those of a clockwork toy.

Dat. Dat-dat-dat. Dat!

With a final cheeky *Drrrrmmmm-dat!* the toy

sank to its knees. But then another clockwork toy came lurching stiff-legged behind and helped it to its feet again.

More shapes followed, and more and more until there were dozens of clockwork toy soldiers staggering about with their arms supporting each other like ghosts dancing.

Sneck laughed with delight as the figures multiplied.

'How's that for a magic spell, you dolts?' he beamed triumphantly. 'Here comes the English army! These are *my* allies and *my* friends, not rats for hire from the gutters of Shrewsbury. Now *you're* in trouble!'

The ruffians gaped. Their mouths opened even further when they saw a green moon on a stick come surging across the courtyard. The colour drained from their faces.

'Oh dear me,' they said. 'Oh dear oh dear oh dear!'

Sybil was also looking out into the courtyard, from the attic window. She too saw the pale green shining moon and her heart swelled with admiration.

'What a wonder!' she cried. 'What a hero! Oh, if only I could find a man like that!'

Bess, peering under Sybil's outstretched arm, felt

extraordinarily happy. 'What a grolyhoomp!' she laughed.

'What a phenomenon!' gasped Sir Simeon.

'HELP!' they shouted.

George, who knew a friend's voice when he heard it, cried 'Be-ee-sss!' at the top of his voice and started an avalanche.

The manor vibrated. Snow tumbled from its roofs.

Inside the great hall the villagers thought an earthquake had begun.

'Save us!' they cried.

George didn't know which way to turn.

Only Solomon Sneck curled his lips in contempt. 'Fools!' he taunted, 'you're all fools!'

In a fit of hysteria he raced to the door, dragged it open and screamed at George:

'*Eeny meeny smidgy small,*
A grolyhoomp's the biggest fool of all!'

George was certainly the biggest something, but he was not in any way a fool. Behind his lost memory he was very wise.

It seemed to him that almost every minute he was learning something new about life on Earth, and

the new thought which came to him now was that in every generation ordinary people were plagued by tyrants who rose to power at the expense of everybody else.

George didn't like that, and he did not in any way like Solomon Sneck, who seemed to him to be as wicked a tyrant as he'd come across in a long while. And now, when everybody should have been helping each other to survive the storm, the sight of that foul-faced, mealy-mouthed, fraudulent magician spouting venom from his sheltered doorway was too much to bear.

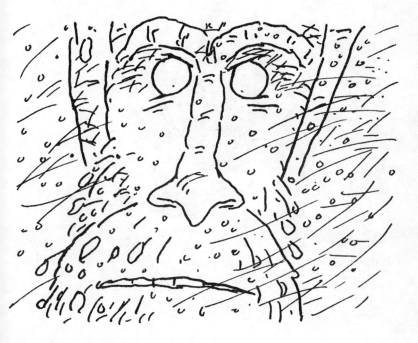

George felt irritated by Sneck, then angry – and then for the first time since he arrived on Earth he got really mad.

Grinding his teeth in fury George snatched up the suddenly shrieking sorcerer in his fist, carried him into the village squirming like one of his own snakes, and stuck him firmly down the tallest chimney of the tallest house in Kingswell.

Naturally, this being the coldest day of the coldest winter for years, there was a massive fire burning down below…

chapter Twenty-Five
Miracle at Kingswell

George was also learning that we humans are subject not only to tyrants but also to our own changeable natures.

The fickle inhabitants of Kingswell were proving that now, because once again the grolyhoomp was a hero and saviour to be cheered to the snowy skies.

They weren't so sure about the army he had rescued but Huw, speaking from George's pocket like a very small preacher in a very large pulpit, explained that the soldiers were far too cold, hungry, frightened, frozen and grateful to be a threat to anybody. What they needed, Huw said, was a little human kindness.

The people looked at the soldiers standing only half alive in the never-ending snow and their hearts melted.

The soldiers looked at the people and, astonished, saw their stony suspicious faces relax and unexpectedly smile. They felt hands which a moment ago had been ready to strike reach out to protect and carry them into the safety of the manor.

It was the first gesture of friendship they had experienced since they left their homes and families a lifetime ago and it was too much. To a man they broke down in tears.

In a moment *everybody* was crying, the people with pity and the soldiers with relief.

Big George watched happily as the spirit of Christmas came at last to Kingswell. He felt moved himself, and liked that feeling so much he wanted to be kind too.

He looked around for things to be kind to – and found five.

Looking down he saw peering from his pocket the two trapped faces of a piglet and a pig boy who were both desperate to reach their families. And looking up he saw three equally pleading faces at a window high up in the manor.

'All right,' George muttered, 'here comes grolyhoomp kindness.'

He pushed a finger through the attic window, pulled the frame out of the wall and poked about inside.

'Bee-eess-sss!' he called.

Whooping with pleasure, Bess wrapped her arms around the great finger and encouraged her father and maid to do likewise.

Sybil flung herself across the first joint. 'What a lark!' she cried. 'What a digit!'

Sir Simeon Griphook gulped nervously and, telling himself that anything his daughter and her maid could do he should be brave enough to do as well, climbed on to the second joint.

Slowly and carefully George withdrew his finger and the three dangling figures entered a crazy world of whirling snow, howling wind and towering drifts.

But there – oh bliss! – was an open door through which a warm light shone and the faces of the whole village beamed an ecstatic welcome.

George put his passengers down in the doorway, then turned and plunged into the blizzard on his second mission of kindness – and on his way to a big surprise.

Christmas Eve was almost over as the grolyhoomp forged through Kingswell's deserted, snowbound streets. Deserted, that is, except for a

lunatic figure waving frantically from a chimney where it was stuck like a cork in a bottle. 'Oooohh!' it shouted, and 'Aaaahh!' as flames leapt up from the hearth below. The figure was also shouting nonsense about frogspit and wormbrains, but George could make no sense of that and didn't want to.

He pressed on.

Soon the village was behind him and in front was the cowshed, its roof sagging under the weight of snow. Huge icicles hung from its eaves and speared the drifts that had built up from the ground. Inside a woman cried out in pain.

Fearing the worst, as soon as Big George had

cleared the doorway and lowered him to the ground Huw ran inside with a thudding heart. The piglet scuttled after him, gurgling with happiness.

What George heard next was a jigsaw of sounds: cows bellowing, horses stamping, pigs excitedly welcoming their prodigal's return – and little Rachel Evans shrieking with joy as she jumped wildly into her brother's arms.

He also heard Sarah Evans gasp, 'Huw! Oh, thank goodness! You're just in time – help me, please!'

After that there was only the moan of the wind and the rustle of falling snow.

George waited.

Hours passed.

Then suddenly the jigsaw was enriched by two cries.

The first was Sarah Evans's shout of triumph.

The second was a thin elongated wail.

George could make no sense of that so he lowered his neck until his face hung upside down outside the cobwebbed window. What he saw inside was truly magical.

In smoky firelight animals were clustering round Huw, who was washing the face of the smallest living person George had ever seen. Rachel gazed at it adoringly and nearby Sarah lay on her pallet, pale but smiling.

'It's a miracle, George. A Christmas gift from Huw's father to his family.' George turned his head and saw Bess standing tiptoe beside him. Then, laughing, she hurried inside.

That was the moment when the snow stopped falling.

It happened quite suddenly, as if a spell had been broken. The wind died, the flakes dwindled and shrank and, as the snow clouds swept away eastward, in the west the stars and moon appeared. The comet dangled its tail above the cowshed and George like a bright chandelier.

In Kingswell, living began again.

Drawn by the comet's brilliant light the villagers left the manor and struggled across the courtyard. Solomon Sneck's thugs, feeling strangely as if a change was coming over them as well as the weather, went with them. 'We have seen his star in the west,' they breathed, 'and we'll never be wicked again.'

Then, thinking that was maybe a little drastic, they told each other not to get carried away. 'After all,' they said, 'it's only a bit of a shine.' But they crossed themselves just in case.

When the people reached the cowshed they saw the Kingswell pig boy, with their lord's daughter by

his side, waiting to greet them. In his arms Huw
held a tightly wrapped bundle.

'It's a boy,' he grinned. 'We're going to call him Little George.'

Big George beamed and stood protectively over them.

'Gg – e – oorr – gg – e', he said. 'Grolyhoomp.'

chapter Twenty-Six

The Spirit of christmas

The villagers, with Sir Simeon Griphook, Sybil and Blind Biffin in front, clustered round the door to the cowshed like an audience at a theatre waiting for the show to begin.

George gave it to them.

He took the icy crown from his own head – how it was still clinging there was a wonder in itself – and placed it on Huw's shaggy locks.

'Kk – ii – nn – gg,' he said.

The people gasped with surprise and muttered among themselves, because of all the strange events which were happening was it not the strangest of all that the lowest among them should become the highest in a single moment?

Yet here was their own lord, Sir Simeon Griphook, falling to his knees and kissing the pig boy's hand and greeting him with, 'Your servant, Sire!'

Bewildering wasn't the word for it!

George had not finished.

Noticing the soldiers he'd rescued tottering at the back of the crowd, he beckoned them to come forward.

Captain Witless, who remained to be convinced that he wasn't dead and this wasn't Judgement Day, cleared his throat nervously.

'Er, on you go, men,' he sniffed. 'Don't hang about. Lead the way, Sergeant Moo.'

The villagers moved aside to let them through.

George regarded the troops very sternly, and pointed to the ground in front of Huw.

'Down we go, boys, and no messing,' said the Captain, throwing himself face down in the snow to show them the way.

The soldiers dropped like skittles and bowed before the Winter King.

Huw gave them a majestic wave.

George now beckoned Sneck's reformed bully boys, who were promising to be sweeter than angels from this moment on if only they were allowed to survive the next few dangerous seconds.

They closed their eyes and pretended not to notice, so George picked them up and dropped them in front of Huw.

They lay down at his feet.

'Sssttt-aaaa-nnndd,' said George.

'Oh lor',' they groaned, standing up and expecting the worst.

To their surprise, Big George very gently took Little George from Bess, held him out to show them, handed him back to Bess and pointed to the cowshed threshold.

'What's that about then?' the ruffians muttered nervously.

'It's very clear to me,' Bess said sternly, 'that the grolyhoomp wants you to guard the baby.'

'Does he?'

Huw smiled. His crown sparkled. 'George does,' he said, and it's the most important job in the world.'

'Oh, well, if you put it like that,' said the reformed thugs, 'we'd be honoured to do it.'

So like a jigsaw the pieces of our story have come together and the picture is complete.

Sir Simeon Griphook has regained his spirit, his village and, most important of all, his dearly loved daughter. He has a new motto: 'Honour the dead but love the living.'

Bess has recovered her father, her future and Huw, her much-loved companion. She has also made a very big and strange new friend.

Huw has altered beyond recognition. He's Winter King, Lord of the Swineherds and, even more exciting, he has a brand-new brother.

The **Soldiers** have their lives when they thought they'd lost them. Drummer William is their hero and Captain Witless their inspiration.

The **Villagers** have a Winter King and Lord to be proud of and a sorcerer they can throw snowballs at any time they feel like it. 'Serves him right,' they say as they pepper him - but they cross themselves just in case.

Solomon Sneck has run out of spells. Wriggle as he might he has become part of a chimney – which, when you think about it, is a better spell than any he managed when he could move around.

Finally, two cowardly ruffians have discovered that they're really quite exceptional characters: brave, bold, intelligent – and angelic. **Sybil** dotes on them.

So honour is satisfied and all's well that ends well.

A grolyhoomp has put a smile on the face of this small corner of the Marchlands and everybody's life has changed because of him.

We will let the good folk of Kingswell resume their interrupted feast and, under the midwinter wandering moon with snow lying deep all around, allow them to eat, sing, and dance the night away.

We can look at them for this last time through the upside-down eyes of a very large grolyhoomp, who smiles fondly at them through the manor window as his feet tap to their music and above his head a dazzling star shines down.

It is, of course, the Christmas star, for at last it is Christmas morning.

chapter Twenty-Seven

Something Has changed

George sees the dancers suddenly shimmer and move away from him. They come back into focus, but he knows what is happening. He's falling asleep again.

It's time to be moving, time to go back to bed. Yawning, he turns away from the manor, steps over the drawbridge and walks into the village.

Pausing among the silent houses he waves to the figure in the chimney, who might have been Santa Claus but isn't. This figure too is nodding with sleep, even though smoke is pouring out of its ears.

When he reaches the little church George pauses again and looks over the wall, where the smooth white expanse of the churchyard glistens under the Christmas moon. Beneath its snowy surface Alice

Griphook is sleeping a very deep sleep, but George doesn't know that. All around, the mountains rear to the starry sky, protecting her.

George marches on.

Half way up the first mountain he turns and looks back, just for a moment, at what he is leaving

behind. Under moon and star Kingswell crouches, a cluster of dark walls and shining roofs. Gleams of yellow light shine from its biggest building and George is sure he can hear the sound of Biffin's harp.

'I should have liked to belong there,' he tells

himself. 'But I can't, and that's that.'

Resolutely he sets off again, and this time he doesn't look back.

But as he climbs, George knows that something is changing inside him.

He's getting to like it here.

afterword

Inside his shelter, Big George sleeps again, with his hands thrust warmly into his coat pockets.

Clasped lightly in his right palm are three lucky charms: a spoon, a rabbit's foot – and a dried up piglet's dropping.

Well, anything can be a gift if it's meant kindly, and you never know when even a piglet's dropping might come in useful.

Life's a pantomime, isn't it?